BLINDED BY FOREVER

NOVELLA

BLINDED BY SERIES

BOOK THREE

JACLIN MARIE

Editing Done by Antonia Salazar from AMS Editing
Cover done by After Dark Cover Designs by Ama

ISBN: 979-8-9916373-7-4

PLAYLIST

CRY	**CIGARETTES AFTER SEX**
STAINED	**SELENA GOMEZ**
BORED	**BILLIE ELLISH**
LET ME IN	**H.E.R.**
I'M YOURS	**ISABEL LAROSA**
LEAVING TONIGHT	**THE NEIGHBORHOOD**
DON'T WANNA CRY	**SELENA GOMEZ**
CHAMPAGNE COAST	**BLOOD ORANGE**
WHERE YOU BELONG	**THE WEEKND**
DANGEROUS HANDS	**AUSTIN GIORGIO**
UNFAIR	**THE NEIGHBORHOOD**
COWBOY	**SELENA GOMEZ**

Blurb

Hayden and Jaclyn have been through so much chaos in their lives that they finally are able to have their happy ending.

But just because they're married, doesn't mean they don't have challenges. Secrets are being hidden as well as feelings.

With two kids and a screaming toddler, life isn't always perfect like the books. While dealing with stress of being parents, going on secret missions, and constantly over-thinking that you aren't good enough, marriages are bound to end in divorce.

The real question is, will Hayden and Jaclyn survive these challenges or push away from one another?

To my readers who have followed Hayden and Jaclyn's journey since my Wattpad days.

One

Jaclyn

Hayden's mouth is heaven, it always has been.

Warm, devoted, and relentless.

It's been more than ten years and I can't get over how good he makes me feel.

I don't even try to hold back the moan that tears out of me, even though the kids should be waking up soon.

But we couldn't help ourselves. I was rubbing my butt against him and he whispered for me to move and lay down.

I didn't ask questions, I just did it because moments like these are rare for us now. The only time we get a moment to ourselves is when the kids are gone at school and River's taking her nap. But most of the time, especially lately, Hayden hasn't really been around.

My legs are thrown over Hayden's shoulders, my fingers tangled in his thick dark hair as he sucks, licks, and kisses me everywhere possible like he had nowhere else to be.

Like his only job today was worshipping me.

"Oh my god, Hayden," I breathed. "You're-"

"Hmm?" he hummed against me, giving me a teasing smirk.

That damn hum vibrated through my spine. I arch off the bed, begging for more.

"Please," I whisper, tightening my fingers in his hair. "Please, don't-"

"Mommy!" The door bursts open and I shoot up so fast I nearly knee Hayden in the face. He yanks the comforter over my waist in one smooth motion while his jaw clenches in frustration. Easton stands at the doorway, his arms crossed over his tiny chest and a pout on his face. "I'm hungry."

Hayden drags his hand over his face and groans. "Easton-"

"I said I'm hungry," he demands, a pout still present on his face.

Hayden looks at me at and I already know what that look says.

Remind me why we decided to have kids.

He rests his head on my lap and holds my waist. I

tangle my fingers through his hair and look at Easton. "We'll be down in five minutes, baby."

He looks between me and his father, his little eye twitching. "You always say that and you just end up staying in bed longer."

"I promise. Go downstairs and we'll be right there," I promise, making Easton stomp down the hallway as he grumbles about waffles.

I pat Hayden's shoulder and he moves off me to lie on his back on the bed. I get up and grab the closest sweater I see. "Your son's got a goddamn alarm clock in his stomach."

"He's your son, too," I mutter while throwing the sweater on. "You gave him the attitude."

Hayden presses his palms over his face, probably mourning the death of our morning sex. I'm sure it'll be awakened by the end of the day like always. Sometimes we're lucky with sex in the morning or throughout the day. But usually Hayden leaves during the day to train or hangout with Killian, even though he said he was done with the Mafia stuff, I still wonder if he is since he talks to Killian and his brother a lot.

"I'm blaming you," he mutters.

I walk over to him and rest my hands on his shoulders. "Blame your timing." I press a kiss to the corner of his lips. "I'm going downstairs to make food for the boys."

"I'll grab River," he mumbles as I walk out of the room and make my way downstairs.

When I round the corner and go into the kitchen I see Junior and Easton.

Junior is on his phone eating a bowl of cereal and Easton is standing with his arms still crossed over his tiny chest with a pout on his face that makes him look like Hayden a little bit.

"That was more than five minutes."

I roll my eyes at him and rest my hand in his hair. "Go watch some cartoons in the living room and I'll make your food quick, I promise." When Easton leaves the kitchen I look at Junior. "You couldn't make a bowl for your brother?" I raise an eyebrow at him.

He stops scrolling on his phone and looks up at me. "He didn't ask." He shrugs.

Fucking kids.

"Mommy!" I hear River scream down the hall as Hayden walks closer to the kitchen.

When he turns the corner, I smile upon seeing River in his arms. She has a big smile on her face and is in her little pink flower pajamas.

Life has gotten crazy since we moved to Italy. Junior is eleven and thankfully his VSD is gone but that doesn't mean he doesn't have check ups, Easton is seven and we had him a little bit after we moved to Italy.

Junior is just like his father as well as Easton although

Easton does have more of my creativity and traits. Junior is moody and barely talks to anyone but that's probably because he is getting older while Easton is loud and will say anything on his mind.

Then we have our little River who we had more than two years ago

She is now almost two years old and full of energy since she's getting closer to her terrible twos stage. She makes a mess wherever she can and I'm not going to lie, I do get frustrated with her just like I did with Easton and Junior.

When I found out I was pregnant I told Hayden after this I was done and didn't want any more children. He loves the kids and says he wants more but the more time that passes by, I see a little bit of the Hayden I knew drain from his eyes which scares me a little bit.

I know Hayden needs time away from the kids, just like I do but lately he's been more busy and rarely home and I don't and will never tell him this but it's starting to take a toll on me, making me overthink and stress.

Hayden goes straight to the coffee machine with River still on his hip. As he passes by he kisses my cheek as I kiss River's cheek.

"Thought you died," Junior says.

"Not yet, kid. That was just your mom screaming."

Blush creeps up on my face and I smack Hayden's shoulder while he smirks.

"Gross!" Junior grimaces.

"Are you making my breakfast mommy?" Easton yells from the living room.

I sigh and Hayden just smiles at me while keeping in a laugh. "Yes, baby. Be patient." I pull out the waffle mix and look at Junior. "Do you want some or was the cereal good?"

"I'll have eggs and bacon. No waffles." I nod my head and get to work.

After Hayden's done making his coffee he leans against the counter, watching the chaos unfold when he lets River go on the floor. She runs to the living room where Easton is dancing to some music on the TV and Junior is still just playing on that damn phone.

I almost regret giving it to him but because he goes to school, I want him to have something to get a hold of me in case of an emergency.

I got a phone around his age so I thought it was fair but I take the phone during dinner or when we're doing a family activity together.

At night I usually make him either read or do his homework and I'll take the phone.

Hayden watches all of the madness unfold and he seems fine, cool, collected, like he enjoys being here and being a family.

Then his phone buzzes on the counter.

I see the change immediately.

His shoulders tighten and there is a spark of distraction in his eyes. He glances down at the screen and his jaw immediately tightens.

He picks it up and sets his coffee down. "Everything okay?" I ask while putting the first waffle on a plate.

"Yea," he says, too quickly if anything. "Just something I have to handle."

My blood freezes and I furrow my eyebrows at him. "Killian?"

Hayden pockets his phone and walks up to me. "Kind of. I'll be back in a couple of hours. I promise," he says, giving me that fake ass smile.

I don't press.

Not yet at least because the kids are here and I don't even know what this is about.

It doesn't always have to be about this Mafia stuff.

Hayden and I have talked about how I think it would be better if he stopped being involved in the Mafia because we have a whole family now and I need to make sure he comes back home to us–to me.

He hides his true emotions as he leans down and presses a kiss to my forehead. "Don't forget about dinner tonight."

His hand slides down my back. "I won't, princess."

Hayden leaves to get ready and comes back down when breakfast is finished. He steals a piece of Junior's bacon before kissing all of the kids' foreheads and my lips. He says bye to all of us and then he's gone.

The front door shuts behind him and I stare at my food while the kids eat and River throws her food around.

I sit there wondering when his promises would stop feeling like they came with an expiration date.

Two

Hayden

Killian's office always smelled like leather and a hint of blood. Not fresh blood though, but the old stench of it that is in the cracks of his wooden floors from the countless of lives he's taken.

The way you can never be free of this life just like the blood never fully leaves from the cracks.

Killian pours glasses of scotch and slides one across the desk to me before leaning back in his chair like he has all the time in the world.

"Someone's stealing from me," he says, sounding so sure of himself.

Most of the time he is.

Lately I've been helping him with some things.

He's been preoccupied with Luna and because her

grandparents passed, he's taken full responsibility over her.

And because of that he asked me to help him with some things for money.

I'm not hurting for cash or anything because I still have my fighting career, I simply am helping him so that I can have some time to myself. Being in a house filled with noise and kids is draining sometimes.

I love Jaclyn, God I do.

But sometimes I just need a break just like Jaclyn needs her breaks to write or have some quiet time to herself.

I told her a while ago I was done with this Mafia bull-shit especially since we have River now, a baby still.

So I should be thinking of my family and what's best for them but deep down, there is a part of me that still wants to have some sort of adrenaline rush. Fighting used to give me that but ever since I started helping Killian, I need more.

"You sure?" I raise an eyebrow at Killian.

Killian gives me a look as if I asked him if water's wet. "The warehouse off of bay 14. Last three shipments came up short, not by much, but enough to make me think someone thinks I'm not paying attention."

I take a slow sip of the scotch. "What are you thinking?"

He shrugs, looking calm as always. "Inside job possibly. This isn't an amateur move, it's subtle, calculated. Someone's bleeding me slowly."

He stands and walks towards his massive wall of windows that overlooks his backyard.

"You want me to dig into it?" I ask, already knowing the answer.

"I want names, faces, motives and I want you to handle it before I have to."

I run a hand down my jaw.

Jaclyn's going to kill me.

She told me not to be involved in this shit and here I am disobeying her, going against her word and potentially putting my family at risk.

I should know better but I don't.

"You think it's someone close?"

"I think," he says, turning back towards me, "that if it is, I need to know now before Luna gets caught in the crossfire."

Killian mentioning his daughter isn't accidental. He plays chess, not checkers.

I nod. "Okay, I'll start with the warehouse manager and move from there." I finish my drink and rise to my feet.

"You're the only one I trust to do this clean," Killian says. "Rowan will meet with you to help out. Said something about brother bonding time."

I roll my eyes because Rowan has been wanting to

catch up for a while but I've been pushing him away since I don't want to add another person on my list telling me what I should and shouldn't do.

I leave Killian's office and check the time on my phone.

I have about three hours before I've got to be home by dinner.

I can make it.

———

The house is dark when I walk in but I know better than to think everyone would be sleeping. Sure enough, the faint glow of a laptop screen glows in the dark of the living room.

I drop my keys onto the counter and kick off my shoes before heading down the hallway.

Jaclyn lays on the couch, her hair in a loose ponytail, her blue light glasses sliding down her nose as she types on her keyboard like her words might vanish from her mind.

She doesn't look up as I walk in.

I lean against the wall across from her, waiting to hear it.

"You missed dinner."

"I know." My voice comes out lower than I expected.

She closes the laptop slowly and takes off her glasses before looking at me.

She doesn't look angry, it's worse.

She looks disappointed. "Again. This isn't the first time, Hayden."

"Got held up."

"Doing what?" She furrows her eyebrows at me, questioning me.

I meet her eyes and feel a knot in my chest tighten. "Stuff with Killian." I kind of tell the truth and she knows it too.

I know she knows that I'm not going to the gym or just hanging out with Rowan and Killian, I'm helping them.

I walk towards the couch and kneel in front of her. She looks down at me, with that same disappointed look in her eyes that is mixed with a little bit of sadness. "I'm sorry. I know I haven't been there for you or the kids a lot lately. I've just been really busy."

"There's no such thing as busy when you have a wife at home, constantly worrying about you and missing you and then three kids who are wondering if their father is coming home that night or even ever."

"Let me make it up to you."

Her eyebrows lift. "How?"

"Let me take you out tomorrow night. Just us. No kids, no distractions. Just you and me."

She studies me, her walls still high. "You're avoiding the conversation."

"I'm asking for one night to make this right," I say quietly. "Please."

Her lips part, like she's about to argue but then sighs. "Fine. But we're still having this conversation. Don't think it's over."

I blow out a mental breath, glad that this is the end for now. I lean in and press a kiss to her neck. "I wouldn't dream of it, princess."

She doesn't smile but she doesn't push me away either.

Which in our world, counts as progress.

Three

Jaclyn

I wore the dress he likes, the one with the open back and it's dark red which makes his eyes darken with want. I curled my hair, which I never do, put on lipstick and even forced myself to forget about the carbs I was about to eat at the Italian restaurant he made a reservation for.

For a while I was feeling excited.

Date nights between Hayden and I were rare.

Between the chaos with the kids, Hayden always leaving for reasons he won't tell me, and then my part-time writing, we barely have time to sit on the couch together, let alone escape into a world where we could pretend that we weren't constantly exhausted.

We took Hayden's black LaFerrari and the drive was

nice. He was going fast and cutting between cars with his hand on my thigh.

But as soon as a message pinged on his phone, his good mood vanished.

Just like it did all the time whenever he got a text and told me he had to leave somewhere.

This whole day we've been spending time with the kids and then as soon as the sitter came, he kissed down my neck, telling me how good I looked before we got into the car.

Ten minutes into the dinner, I knew something was up. He was quiet. Too quiet.

He wasn't the smirking Hayden I'd dressed up for. He wasn't holding my hand across the table or smiling at me.

It made me feel like something was wrong with me.

Like I wasn't good enough.

He made me feel exactly how I felt in high school.

But I won't cry in front of him because the Hayden who's been sleeping next to me isn't the same Hayden that I fell in love with and gave a second chance to.

I sip my wine and try to make conversation with him again. "So, Junior's math teacher emailed me today."

"Yea?" he asks, his eyes flicking towards me before going back to his plate.

"Yea, apparently, he's been helping other kids understand the homework. She said that she's never seen someone his age explain things so clearly."

This would be the time where he says something like, he got his smarts from me or make a joke out of it but all he does is nod.

It was the kind of nod that meant he wasn't really listening.

And I felt my heart crack.

I wore this dress and got ready for him.

Just so he can see me.

Does he still love me?

Are the messages on his phone someone else?

Does he not want me anymore?

Does he want to throw me away like I'm some toy he's bored of?

Is he finally done with me?

Was I not enough?

What did I need to do to make him see me?

I was fine with losing him all those years ago but now, I can't lose him.

Not when I have three kids with him and he's the only one who knows how deep my scars truly run.

I swear I was close to tearing up but then the waiter came by with the check.

Hayden takes care of it and when the waiter comes back with his card, we leave the restaurant and drive home.

During the drive, Hayden doesn't put his hand on my thigh as he drives back. He drives at a faster speed, like he's angry and just wants to go home already.

The weight of everything he didn't say felt like it was crushing in my chest.

I had enough.

I couldn't do this anymore.

When the front door closed behind us, I turned to face him. "What's going on with you?"

"Not tonight, Jaclyn," he mutters as he pulls his jacket off.

Saying my name.

Not princess or Jackie.

Just with a cold and dismissive tone.

"No," I cross my arms over my chest. "You don't get to check out all night, lie to me about what's going on with you, change the subject multiple times, and make me feel like shit. You've been off for weeks, ever since you started disappearing. Coming home late. Lying!"

He turns, eyes flashing. "I'm not lying."

I scoff. "Bullshit.

He walks towards me. "You don't understand. You won't."

"Then help me understand!" I shout, forcing the tears to go down as I basically beg him for more. "You said this was behind us!"

"It's not that simple."

"Yes, it is! You keep walking away from me and making me feel like complete shit like I'm not enough for you."

He looks at me like I'm crazy.

Like I'm crazy for feeling like this. "When I have I ever fucking said that?" He raises his voice.

"You didn't have to say anything, Hayden. You show it through your actions. Nodding when I'm trying to make conversation with you, always leaving all day and not returning home for dinner, checking your phone for messages, not looking at me!" I can't stop the tears from my eyes. "I know you'd never cheat Hayden but why does it feel like you are? Your job or whatever you're doing with Killian and Rowan, you're cheating on me with that because for some reason, the Hayden I fell in love with, isn't coming home."

He shakes his head. "Don't do that. I don't mean to make you feel like that, it's just I'm trying to protect you."

"I didn't ask you to protect me! I asked you to be here!"

The silence that follows is deafening and we stare at each other, both breathing heavily. I can't help the tears that fall and I wipe them away. "Shit," I say, feeling embarrassed for crying in front of my own husband.

"Mommy?" We both turn at the same time. Easton is standing at the first step of the stairs holding his tiger stuffed animal while rubbing his tiny fists against his eyes. "Why are you yelling?"

Shit.

I walk up to him and pick him up to hold him up to

my waist. "I'm sorry, baby. We didn't mean to wake you." He looks past me to Hayden, confusion written all over his face. "Let's get you back to bed, okay?" He nods and buries his face in my neck.

As I carry him upstairs I look back once.

Hayden stands there, jaw clenched, hands in fists at his sides.

And the moment I'm out of sight, I hear the front door open.

And close.

Hard.

Four

Hayden

The house is quiet when I get back.

Too quiet.

It's the kind of silence that makes you feel like you don't belong in your own home.

I stand in the hallway for a second, letting the weight of everything sink in. My fists still ache from how tightly I clenched them. My jaw too. From holding back all the things I didn't say earlier.

I never wanted to yell at her. Not Jaclyn but, fuck, I was stretched so thin I felt like I might snap straight down the middle.

Whenever I get a message from Killian, I can't help but go into some sort of protective zone or something. Like I can't show or tell anything to Jaclyn in order to protect her.

The message from Killian during dinner, I didn't expect it. He sent me more information on the person who is possibly stealing from him and Rowan hasn't stopped blowing up my phone. I felt overwhelmed and then I had my beautiful wife, sitting in front of me waiting for me to notice her.

I drop my keys on the counter and head upstairs.

I go into River's room first, checking on her. She's sleeping snuggly in her little princess bed that I built for her. She is holding a Simba stuffy against her chest. Her mouth is parted as she snores loudly.

I move a strand of hair away from her face and lean down to press a gentle kiss to her forehead. She looks so much like her mother with the soft brown eyes and long brown hair. She is a creative kid and has such a wild imagination like Jaclyn.

I leave River's room and check on Junior who is right across from River's. Junior has one leg out of his bed and he is completely sprawled out on the bed. His night lamp is on because he's secretly scared of the dark but he will always act like tough shit.

His room is a mess like always even though Jaclyn and I tell him all the time to clean up after himself.

I leave his room and go to check on Easton who heard Jaclyn and I yelling.

When I open the door and look inside I notice his bed is full.

My stomach sinks as I see Jaclyn holding Easton in the little twin sized bed, holding our son like he was the last bit of peace she had left. I walk closer to them and notice her tear stained cheeks and that her eyes are puffy.

My heart fucking breaks.

All I could think about when I left was how I made her feel.

I made her feel like she wasn't enough, like she needed to be better or look better and that's the worst feeling especially after knowing everything she went through.

Jaclyn went through hell and back and she did it all alone when I should have been there for her. She's there for everyone but when is someone going to be there for her?

I was supposed to be the person she can hold onto and always go to whenever things are too hard to carry. I was supposed to be there to help her through everything and I ended up being the thing she started crying about.

I move quietly and pick her up, the way I have hundreds of times before.

She stirs against me. "H-Hayden?"

"Yea, it's me," I whisper as I carry her out of the room and close the door behind me.

Her arms loop lazily around my neck as I carry her back to our room. She doesn't protest, just sighs and rests her head against my chest, like even half asleep, she needed me close.

I lay her down on the bed and sit beside her, brushing her hair away from her face. She looks at me, half asleep but slowly waking up. "I'm sorry I made you feel like that. That's the last thing I want to make you feel."

"Then why did you?"

I sigh before raking my fingers through my hair. "I didn't realize that I was pushing you away while trying to also protect you."

"You need to stop doing that." Jaclyn sits up and wraps the blanket around her. "I've survived the worst, Hayden. All I need is you, all I want is you. The only reason I was able to survive what I did is because I knew you were waiting for me but what's the point of you protecting me or us when you won't be there afterwards?" I look at her, really look at her and see what she's carrying. The weight of another possible lie, the weight of taking care of the kids by herself when I'm not here. "You've been lying to me. We're supposed to be partners Hayden and tell each other things but it feels like I've been doing all this by myself."

"I know, I'm sorry. Killian... he's having some issues and he needs me to help."

"Will you helping him cause me to lose you though? You have your own family and that should always come first."

I rest my hand on her knee. "I know, princess. I'm sorry. It's just..." I sigh and rake my hands through my hair again. "It's just that I needed a break and Killian was there and I got in too deep again with the wrong people. Now he needs help and I couldn't say no." Her face falls but she doesn't interrupt. "Someone's been stealing from him. He wants me to handle it and figure it out. I didn't want to because I knew what this would mean."

"Why didn't you just tell me the truth instead of lying to me? You think I like telling the kids that I don't know where you are? They aren't blind, they see what's happening too."

"I know," I say, my voice low. "I thought I'd lose you if I told you. I thought it would drive a wedge between us."

She reaches for my hand, threading her fingers through mine. "You don't lose me by telling the truth, you lose me by keeping secrets."

I pull her closer and rest my forehead against hers. "It's just this one last thing. Once I help him figure it out, I'm done. I swear."

Her breaths hitch and for a long second, we just sit there in the silence between heartbeats.

Then Jaclyn leans forward and kisses me.

Soft, slow, like a quiet forgiveness.

I cup her face, deepening the kiss, letting everything I couldn't say bleed through my hands, my mouth.

I trail one of my hands down her body and hold her thigh, grabbing her to pull her onto my lap.

Her legs wrap around me and my hands start to slowly

slide under her shirt as the kiss turns hungry, desperate, like we were making up for every second lost to silence.

I grab her shirt and rip it off her. I lean down and take her nipple in my mouth. She holds my head against her chest as she grinds into me, my erection growing hard beneath her. I lick and suck her nipple in my mouth. She grips my hair in her hands and moans.

I switch over to the next one as she slides her hands down to undo my belt.

Our clothes are ripped off from each other and I pull her back on my lap and hold her against me as she slowly slides down my shaft.

When I finally sink fully inside her, it feels like coming home.

There was no space between us, no anger, or lies.

"Oh, Hayden," she moans, gripping my hair.

I lean towards her and kiss her, all the thoughts and worries disappear as I move inside her. She rocks against me, getting faster with every motion.

I didn't apologize to her with my words anymore. I apologized with my hands gripping her hips like she'll disappear with every breathless groan of her name on my lips.

We kiss passionately and I grip her ass in my hands, moving her on me.

"I love you so much," I whisper against her lip.

She clenches around me and presses a hard,

demanding kiss on my mouth. She can have all the kisses she wants. She can steal every single kiss from my mouth until I have nothing left and I'll be okay.

"I love you," she whispers back.

My cock tenses inside her and like her body knows, she tightens around me. I slam inside her and hold her against me as I spill my seed inside her.

She shivers and moans while on top of me.

All I can think about as we both finish at the same time is Jaclyn.

Just Jaclyn. My life, my everything.

And me, clinging to her like she was the only thing keeping me alive.

Because in a way she was.

Always has been and always will be.

Five

Jaclyn

My hand touches the space next to me, trying to feel for Hayden but his side of the bed is cold.

It takes me a moment to register that the spot beside me is empty. His scent lingers in the sheets but it's cold.

I blink the sleep from my eyes as sunlight peeks through the curtains.

Things between Hayden and I have been better since we argued. He's communicating as much as he can with me about things with Killian. He doesn't tell me the specifics or what kind of stuff Killian wants him doing but he's telling me where he is instead of just saying he's leaving for the day and not telling me where he's going.

I can tell he's trying, for us, for the kids. For our forever like we both promised each other. The tension that hung over us for the last few days had finally started to loosen.

I slip out of bed and pull on one of Hayden's old t-shirts. It smelled like him, musk and clean soap as well as a hint of his cologne that he carries around in his scent with him.

I head down the stairs and towards the kitchen where I hear voices.

Little ones and then a louder one, deep, warm, and teasing.

I lean against the doorway and watch for a moment.

Hayden stands at the stove, barefoot in just sweatpants showing off his ripped body, that he perfectly created himself with good nutrition and constant workouts in the gym. He's flipping pancakes while Junior is sitting at the island with a juice box. Easton is dancing in his pajamas with River twirling around, laughing.

I smile because I love seeing our madness and chaos, the life that Hayden and I created together when there were no arguments or issues about coming home late at night.

I walk in and he immediately turns his head to look at me. "You didn't wake me up."

A spark flickers in his eyes as I walk towards him. He wraps his arms around me and presses his lips to mine. "I didn't want to. You never get to sleep in so I thought I'd take care of breakfast today." I smile up at him. "You want pancakes, eggs, and bacon?"

"Yes."

Once Hayden finishes cooking and I set the table putting in my units for my OMI-Pod, we all sit down together. River is in her tiny chair sitting between Hayden and I. Her face is sticky with syrup and I know for a fact she's going to need a bath after this, she always does. Easton is arguing with Junior about some random video game that they play together.

I catch Hayden's eyes at one point and he's smiling while looking at our chaos. He looks happy, content, like the Hayden who wasn't gone all the time and was more involved.

"I'm going to take the boys to school today before heading to Killian's," Hayden announces after the boys finish their food and leave the table. "It'll give you some time to write while River takes her nap." He gets up and takes both of our plates.

I smile at him. "Really?"

"Yea, you deserve some quiet time."

That meant a lot, him taking some weight off my shoulders and taking the boys to school and picking them up. I haven't been able to write much because of the constant overthinking I've been doing about Hayden. It feels good to be able to have a moment to write without the craziness happening in the background.

Hayden grabs River to take a bath with her so that he can get ready as well while I clean up the mess downstairs and do the dishes.

By the time I finish cleaning up, the boys are ready for school and Hayden is walking downstairs in navy trousers and a white dress shirt. He's holding River whose hair is wet from her bath with Hayden.

"Mommy! Hold!" she cheers, reaching towards me.

I grab her from Hayden and kiss her cheek, making her giggle. "You're so clean. You're not a sticky baby anymore."

Hayden smiles at us and he grabs my cheek, stroking my skin softly. "I'll be back to pick up the boys from their sports and then we can have dinner as a family."

"Perfect."

He leans towards me and pecks me on the lips. "I love you," he mumbles against my lips.

And for a second, for those good few hours, it felt like everything was back to normal. We were back to our normal.

"I love you." He smiles against the kiss before I lean away. "Go before you guys are late."

"I'll see you, princess." He walks towards the front door, grabbing the X6 M car key. "Boys!" he yells, before walking out the door. "Let's go or I'm leaving without you."

"Bye, mom," the boys say as they run past me out the door.

River and I watch them leave out the estate gate before the Sport SUV roars down the street. River and I go back inside the house and head to the living room. I put a movie on for River to watch so that I can write in peace.

I write one good chapter before she starts crying, which means that she needs her nap.

It's the middle of the day and that's usually when she takes her naps. I carry River to her crib and gently tuck her in. I brush a few strands of hair from her face and turn on the white noise in her room.

When I get back downstairs I turn on the baby monitor as I start writing again. After I stopped working as a sports journalist turned into a full-time mom, I decided to take up writing.

I have published one book and it did really well. Most of the books I write are self help books. I talk about my experiences in my life, having Type 1 diabetes, what I went through in college, my overthinking, and just mental health in general.

It's helped me a lot, more than I thought it would. It's my form of therapy ever since I canceled services with my old therapist.

Words poured out in steady lines, the kind of focused flow I haven't felt in weeks.

Everything made sense.

All of the readers who have read my books, they all said they finally found someone and a story that they can relate to and it makes me feel good knowing that sharing my story or feelings can help other people.

By the time I finish the third chapter of the day, I hear a faint scream from upstairs and a sound coming from River's baby monitor.

I look at the time and see it's been a good two hours. I lost track of time.

I get off the couch and run upstairs towards her room, almost slipping from turning the corner. I turn on the lights in her room and look at her face.

She is sitting up in bed, face red, tears streaking down her cheeks. She looks terrified–like the kind of scared that only a nightmare can pull from a toddler.

"Hi, baby," I whisper as I lean down to grab her into my arms.

Her fingers cling onto my shirt. "Mommy," she sobs, hiccuping. "Bad bird..."

My heart clenches.

She's definitely my kid because one fear I never got over when I was a kid was birds. I'm absolutely terrified of them, always will be.

"I've got you, River. You're safe."

She tucks her head under my chin and her tears soak the fabric of my shirt. I rock her gently and sit down on the floor with her in my arms.

I stay there for a while, just holding her and humming softly.

When I was pregnant with River, she was my first girl so I was worried. I thought I was going to be like my mother and that was a worry I mentioned to Hayden.

Hayden reassured me that I was a great mom to Easton and Junior and I was going to be an even greater mom to River.

I never thought I would love these kids as much as I love myself but I do. They are all I think about and I can't imagine what I would do if someone were to hurt them.

That's why I think I'm so strict about Hayden being here because I want to experience this with him and if he's out helping Killian, there is always a possibility of death for him and I can't afford to lose him.

Only reason I'm where I'm at today is because of him.

Six

Jaclyn

It's hard to enjoy dinner when I know it's starting again.

River is laughing and making a mess per usual, Easton is trying to tell me about his day at school, and Junior has the same look I have in my eyes as he constantly looks down the hallway to where the front door is, wondering if his dad is going to show up or not for another family dinner he missed this week.

We were doing good, I don't know what happened or how we got here.

I'm feeling the silence.

The small shift happening between him and our family.

I'm feeling anxious about him not coming home at the time he said he would.

For a week, things between us were fine but then Killian started asking for him more. He started coming home late at night this week, but in the beginning he would text me. But tonight, I haven't gotten one single text from him.

All week he has been with Killian and at least before, he would have days off to spend time with me or the kids but it feels like we only see him in the morning and then he's gone.

"Mommy," Easton says, moving his plate towards me. "Can I have more mashed potatoes?"

"Of course, baby." I force a smile and scoop some mashed potatoes on his plate. I look back at Junior who stares at the door again, like he expected Hayden to walk through with his arms wide and a big smile on his face.

But the door stayed closed.

"Where's dad at?" Junior finally asks.

I hesitate, my throat tightening. "He's with Luna's dad. Work stuff."

Another lie.

Another cover I wasn't sure I could keep telling.

Junior is old enough to understand the shift between us and Hayden pulling back.

After we're all done eating our food, the boys help me clean up while I clean up River's chair and her mouth. Now that the boys are older, they help around the house whenever they can or whenever I tell them too.

I want to be proud that they are helping me without me asking but it's hard when all I'm thinking about is their father's whereabouts and whether he's coming home or not. Usually I go to sleep and ignore it but the more I do, the more it's all bugging me and becoming too much.

Once we're all done cleaning up, I send the boys upstairs to wash up for bed. I bring River to my and Hayden's bathroom so that I can take a bath with her. Hayden and I always end up just showering with her because she makes a mess in the tub and water ends up going everywhere.

After River's bath, I read her a bedtime story and she knocks out after the first few pages. For Easton, I put on the little song machine he has in his room because it helps him fall asleep. Junior has his night lamp on and I'm about to close the door but he stops me.

"Is dad coming home?"

My heart cracks a little bit.

I don't know but I can't say that to him.

I don't want to make Hayden look bad because Hayden isn't a bad dad, he just makes bad decisions that are reckless and sometimes selfish.

I walk into his room and sit on his bed. "Yea, he just got held up but I'm sure he'll be home soon."

"He's been gone a lot lately." I don't say anything because I can't. Everything I want to say, I can't say to

Junior. I don't want Junior to see his father as a bad guy. "You guys have been fighting a lot too."

"Adults fight. It's normal." I rub his shoulder and lean towards him to press my lips against his forehead. "Get sleep, you have school tomorrow."

I get up and as I'm about to walk out, Junior says, "Love you, mom."

"Love you, too." I force a smile on my face as I close his bedroom door.

I go downstairs to the living room and turn on some random show. Even though my laptop is on the coffee table in front of me I don't even try to write.

I just wait.

An hour passes.

Another hour long episode plays.

And by the time I hear the front door creak open it's 1 in the morning.

I turn towards the entryway and see him.

He closes the door behind him as he stands tall, broad, and tired.

I look down at his hands, they are red. The knuckles scraped raw and skin torn in places, blood dripping from the cuts on his hand. His shirt has smudges too, dark and angry.

"Are you serious right now?" I stand slowly.

He freezes like he didn't expect me to be awake and wait for him. "Princ-"

"Don't princess me." I storm towards him. "What the hell is going on with you? You're coming home late again, barely seeing the kids or me, and walking in our home like this?"

"I didn't mean to scare you," he says, low and firm. "It wasn't supposed to go this far…"

"But it did. And you didn't even call or text that you were coming home. You left me here by myself with the lies I had to tell the kids. When River cried and asked where her daddy was I had to tell her that he'll be home soon when I didn't even know if that was true or not. Easton, when he was done with his shower, asked why you were still gone. Or Junior when he kept looking at the door during dinner to see if you'd show up," I say, as tears build in my eyes. "I can't keep doing this Hayden."

"I told you, I'm handling something for Killian. It shouldn't be long before this is all done. It's temporary."

"Temporary?" I raise an eyebrow at him. "That's always what you tell me. But when is this temporary shit going to make you see that it's also putting us in danger? Did you forget what happened? Did you forget what I had to go through?"

His eyes darken. "Don't bring that up."

"I will bring it up, Hayden, because the shit you're in right now is way worse than it was with Eric and Marco because this time it's the Mafia and you have three children living under your roof!"

"I knew I should've never fucking told you." He shakes his head.

"And lie to me?"

"If I lied to you, at least I'd be somewhat protecting you. It's better when you don't know anything. You think I want this? That I want to walk around with blood on my hands?" he shouts, his voice echoing off the walls.

I stare at him, my heart pounding hard in my chest.

How did we even get here?

How did it get this bad?

We were doing fine.

"I'm not mad that you're bleeding, Hayden. I'm mad that you didn't think I could handle the wounds. I don't care what the reasons are. I care that you're pulling away from us, from me." I point to my chest. "Imaging how I feel when the kids ask me where their father constantly is. You're making me feel exactly how I felt when you first started doing this shit, Hayden, and I can only take so much." He steps forward but I step back. "I can't do this tonight. I'm tired of how many fucking times I have to tell you."

I turn and go up the stairs, not waiting for his reply.

Behind me I hear him punch a wall and I swear I felt that punch in my heart as a sob breaks through. I don't look back or go downstairs.

I climb into bed and pull the blanket over my body even though I know sleep won't come easy.

This isn't the first time I've felt alone in this house but somehow it still hurts just as much.

Seven

Hayden

When I open my eyes I see Jaclyn's back to me. Her bare shoulder peeking from beneath the sheets like an invitation I didn't deserve.

The room was quiet but birds were chirping from the open window. I can hear her OMI-Pod clicking as it delivers insulin to her body.

She got on the OMI-Pod a few years ago and it's been a life changer for her. She still uses the shots whenever she can't refill her prescription for the pod but her blood sugars are a lot better ever since she started using that device.

After I cleaned myself up last night and washed the blood off my hands, I slid into bed next to her and pulled her close to me. She was sleeping so she turned around and snuggled into me as if I didn't make her cry. I held her like she was mine, but the truth is, I broke her in ways I can't fix.

I stare at her longer than I should've. Her face was turned slightly in the pillow, her eyes puffy from crying and lips parted.

"Your job or whatever you're doing with Killian and Rowan, you're cheating on me with that because for some reason, the Hayden I fell in love with, isn't coming home."

Her words echo in my head as I drag my hand down my face and slip out of the bed, careful not to wake her up.

I go to the bathroom and get ready for the day quickly. I put ointment on my hands and dress in black jeans and a shirt.

Before I leave the bedroom I take one last look at Jaclyn and my heart clenches.

How did it all get down to this? How did we get so far from each other?

It's because of me.

I open the bedroom door and leave Jaclyn to sleep while I get the kids ready for school.

Fear creeps up my neck as I think about the future.

Fear that I'm screwing this up, again.

When I get to the kitchen, Junior is sitting at the table, slouched over a bowl of cereal, tapping his spoon against the edge of the bowl in a steady rhythm.

He looks up at me with too-old eyes. I didn't realize how fast he's growing up until now.

As he stares at me like I'm guilty of something.

And I am.

I wish I never started helping Killian again.

"You and mom were yelling last night."

I pause, not because I didn't expect it, but because I have no idea how to answer that without lying to my son.

And I was tired of lying and letting Jaclyn take the heat for everything I'm doing. "Yea." I move towards the coffee machine. "We were."

"Are you guys gonna get a divorce?" he asks, straight up.

The mug in my hands almost slips. "What? No. Jesus, Junior."

"You sounded like you hated each other."

As I look at Junior I notice how scared he looks. My heart twists, sharp and sick.

"I don't hate your mom." I rest the coffee mug on the counter and walk over to him. "I could never hate your mom. I love her but sometimes we fight. I wish you hadn't heard that but I promise you it doesn't mean that we're not okay. You hear me?" Junior nods slowly but I can tell my explanation wasn't good enough. "We're gonna be okay. I'm just doing something you're mom doesn't like."

"Then why don't you stop?"

"It's hard. The work I'm in doesn't allow me to leave so easily but I'm going to try." I put my hand on his shoulder. "For you, for your brother and your sister. Most importantly for your mom."

He nods again and looks down at his cereal bowl like it betrayed him for turning soggy. I ruffle his hair and go to make coffee.

Easton comes in ten minutes later demanding pancakes. I make a quick batch for him, Junior, and an extra two for River and Jaclyn for when they come down for breakfast.

After they are finished eating, they clean up and do their dishes. By the time we leave the house, Jaclyn hasn't come downstairs and River is still sleeping, surprisingly. I debated going upstairs to check on Jaclyn but I know if I did I wouldn't want to leave.

The boys decide to take the M4 out today. Junior calls shotgun and Easton pouts but goes in the backseat.

Their school isn't that far, only about a ten minute drive.

After I drop them off I drive straight to Killian's house. The estate is quiet when I pull up which is odd since his house is always always alive with Luna's laughter.

When I walk in, Luna's toys are scattered on the floor and the smell of coffee brewing fills my senses.

I walk towards Killian's office.

He's holding a cup of coffee and a phone against his ear as he paces the room back and forth. He looks up at me and immediately hangs up and gestures for me to sit down.

I sit in front of his desk and he comes around to sit in his chair. "I need you to go to California."

"No," I say without hesitation.

Killian raises an eyebrow at me. "Excuse me?"

"You heard me. I'm not going to California. This shit is pulling me away from my family."

Killian leans towards me. "Who's the one that came to me for a job in the first place? Asking for some sort of adrenaline because the calm life is getting boring for him?"

"And I realize the mistake I made. I found the person who is stealing from you like you wanted me to and now I want to be out. Jaclyn's literally holding onto me by a thread and I don't want to lose her."

He studies me and for a moment something shifts in his expression, like he understands.

But it passes.

"I need someone I can count on, Hayden." He says, his voice turning calmer, steadier like he is trying to be careful with his words. "If it's not you, I can find someone else but if that someone were to fuck it up then you and I both know what kind of war will start and who would be caught in the crossfire."

I clench my jaw.

He's right and he fucking knows it.

Smart bastard knows how to play his cards right and that's all thanks to his father.

I've only met his father, Ace De Luca, once and I realize where Killian got all of his traits from.

When I met Ace, it was over a family dinner that I was invited to because Rowan is married to someone in the family and Killian was my best-friend and boss.

Ace is everything that everyone says he is.

Cold, controlled, and selfish or at least that last part is what Killian says.

Killian has a thing against his father, everyone can tell. During the dinner Killian was very passive aggressive with Ace and vise versa.

"You used to love doing this. Now you act like it's poison," he adds.

"It is poison," I mutter, "and I think I've swallowed enough."

Killian finishes his coffee and sets his mug down. "You go to California. Handle this as quick and clean as possible. When you come back we can discuss what's next for you."

I pause because a part of me wants to just walk away from all of this and listen to Jaclyn. I want to be there for my family.

But part of me wants the adrenaline, it craves the danger and violence.

"I'll go but I swear after this I can't do this anymore. Even if I ask you, I need you to shove me away. I need to stop this and not put myself in this position."

"Your brother has been bugging me about it so trust me, I'll leave you alone, Hayden. I don't want issues with my family." He gives me a look that I can relate to.

Eight

Jaclyn

I toss and turn in bed before slowly waking up. Hayden's side of the bed is empty and cold but it still smells like him, confirming he did sleep here last night.

I turn and stare up at the ceiling for a long minute, jaw clenched and breath held. Even though the fight was last night I feel like we haven't had a proper conversation for a while, like we're not even close to being connected like the way we were before.

No doubt the blood on his hands came from one of Killian's victims but I don't know what's going on and why Hayden won't communicate with me anymore.

I'm trying to go through all the recent memories of Hayden and I to figure out how we got to this point and what changed.

I force myself up and to shower, washing away all of

the overthinking and the dangerous thoughts running through my brain.

When I'm done I throw on leggings and one of Hayden's baggy sweaters.

His scent makes the ache in my stomach stronger but I ignore it.

I pass by River's room and see that she's still sleeping. Her cheeks are flushed and her curls are in a tangled mess. Drool is falling from her parted lips as she snores.

It's about 9 in the morning so I'm surprised that she is still asleep. She usually wakes up around the same time as the boys because of all the noise they make in the morning.

Downstairs, the boys are already gone.

Hayden must've taken them to school this morning.

I make myself coffee and eat the pancake that Hayden left for me. There is one also set aside for River.

I silently eat breakfast with my phone face down on the counter.

There was no text or call from Hayden.

An hour goes by and River wakes up crying. So I rush upstairs to her. I hold her against my waist and rock her, trying to calm her down.

"You're okay baby. Looks like it's just me and you today again." I smile and kiss the side of her head.

She clings onto me as I go downstairs to the kitchen. I put River in her chair and heat up her pancake while also heating up a bottle of milk for her.

River babbles about everything and anything while she makes a mess as per usual.

Easton and Junior weren't this messy when they were babies. River is definitely my wild child out of my kids but I love her and her mess.

"What do you wanna do today, baby?" I ask before opening the fridge. "We can go grocery shopping and maybe buy some stuff for the kitchen?" I ask her as if she'll answer me.

A little sunshine and fresh air would be good for us instead of just staying in the house all day.

After River is done with her breakfast I give her a quick bath and put on a cute little outfit for her to wear.

While I grab my purse and keys she walks around, touching everything she can in the hallway.

Ever since she started walking, all she's been doing is wanting to walk around and reach up to touch things.

I grab my diaper bag for River, since she is still potty training, and some snacks in case she gets hungry. I buckle her in her carseat in the X6 M. Usually I take this car whenever we or I go out with River since this is the only car with a carseat for her. We could put her in the M4 but because that car is a coupe it's a little difficult.

When we get to the grocery store, it doesn't look that packed, thank God. I grab River out of her carseat and put her in the cart. River hums to herself while chewing her snacks.

She was already demanding more food when we were on our way to the store probably because she wasn't even eating breakfast. She was more like throwing it all over the floor.

We didn't need much from the grocery store. Just a few snacks, fruits, and fresh produce.

River points to all kinds of snacks she wants and even sees a dinosaur stand that is advertising some cereal. "Rawr!" she yells before giggling, like it's the funniest thing in the world.

I smile down at her even though that smile doesn't reach my eyes. I try though, for her and for the rest of my family to pretend that things are okay between me and Hayden even though things aren't.

As I look through the fresh produce my phone in my pocket buzzes. For a second I think it might be Hayden until I see Rowan's name pop up on the caller ID.

I hesitate for a moment before answering. "Hey."

"Hey." His voice was familiar, reminding me of Hayden's voice. "You sound tired."

I don't talk to Rowan much unless it's about Hayden. You can tell that Rowan really cares for his family, especially Hayden since he is the youngest sibling in his biological family.

Over the years Hayden has grown closer with his

biological siblings while also still making time for the family that raised him over the years. Sometimes Alex and Carter will visit with Natalia and Chris.

"I am," I admit.

"Hayden?"

"Who else?" I try to laugh but it comes out dry. "He's back to disappearing again. Late nights with blood on his hands. Vague answers. I'm trying to be patient and let him finish his job but I'm starting to feel like I'm married to a ghost."

"I know. I'm trying to talk to him about this but he isn't answering my calls." Rowan sighs over the phone. "Have you talked to him?"

"I did but he just shuts down and avoids it. We had a huge fight last night because he came home late with blood on his hands and shirt. I have no clue what I'm supposed to do."

"He always had a habit of shutting people out when shit gets heavy, especially you, since he never wants to worry you or make you scared because of your guys' past. He's not shutting you out because he doesn't love you, that would never be the case. But, he thinks he's protecting you by not pulling you in."

"I was in the moment I met him. He shouldn't push me away or shut me out, that's just what made things worse between us. I just want the truth and for things to go back to normal. I want Hayden to be home and spend time with me and the kids."

"You're right. I told him this when he started helping Killian again. I told him to remember that he has a family to come home to every single night and to not take it for granted. That's why I'm pulling away because I have Jane and the kids I need to worry about. I need to focus on protecting my family." Rowan's voice softens. "He thinks he's protecting you by keeping you out of it and pushing his problems away from you but he needs a reason to stop."

"I'm not going to give up."

"That's good. If you were, then you wouldn't be talking to me about it while spending the day with your daughter." I smile a little as I push the cart around the store. "He's not cheating on you," Rowan says, almost like he needs me to hear it. "I know that's not where your head went but if it did, don't let it stay there."

"I know, I never thought he was but it feels like he is whenever he is gone and not paying attention to me and the kids. I'm starting to feel invisible to him."

Rowan pauses for a while before saying. "He loves you. He's just scared of losing you and sometimes fear makes him do stupid shit."

I nod even though he can't see me.

"Mommy, look!" River points to something and I smile at her while nodding my head.

"Thanks for calling, Rowan."

"Always. You love and care about my brother. You're considered my family too. Call me if you need anything. I'm going to talk to Hayden."

We get off the phone as River starts to whine about me not giving her attention.

She's just like me.

Maybe Hayden is scared but so am I.

I'm scared of losing the man I've loved since college and that he's slowly starting to fade into the background and I won't be able to get him back.

Nine

Hayden

When it was time for Killian to put Luna to bed, I saw myself out.

This whole day Killian has just been going over what I'll be doing in California and my arrangements for when I get there. He said I shouldn't be there long, two to three days at the most if everything goes well.

I don't want to and I tried to tell him I need to get out of this, but he just hung shit over my head. Like I can't live without the rush or the adrenaline. I needed some sort of stimuli in order not to go crazy.

By the time I pull into my estate, it's hitting 9. The lights inside are all mostly turned off except for the one in my and Jaclyn's bedroom.

Jaclyn is still awake, of course.

Probably writing since that's what she does whenever she has a flicker of alone time which hasn't been much because of how much I've been gone.

The kids are probably all in bed by now since their bedtime is 8 p.m..

I didn't mean to stay this long, again. I never do but sometimes Killian's meetings run over or an issue comes up that Killian sends me to fix.

The wounds on my knuckles reopened, they started bleeding a little bit from how I'm clenching and unclenching my fists constantly throughout the day.

I lock my car when I get out of it and walk through the front door of our house. The house is quiet, the kind of thick, eerie quiet that says more than yelling ever could.

I walk upstairs to my and Jaclyn's room, passing by the kids' rooms and just going straight to her.

When I open the door softly, Jaclyn is sitting on the bed with her legs crossed, wearing one of my old t-shirts and a sad look on her face as she types on her laptop.

She doesn't look up at me as I close the door behind me.

"Hey," I say as I take off my shoes.

Nothing.

Her fingers tap against the keys, but slower now. More like she is pretending to focus.

I unzip my jacket and let it fall onto the bench. I move

towards the bathroom and catch myself in the mirror. Messy hair from how many times I've run my hand through it. My hands scraped with blood from the wounds that reopened.

"You're bleeding again." Her voice finally breaks the silence. I don't answer right away. I just walk towards the bathroom and start washing away the blood. "Hayden."

"I'm fine," I mutter.

"That's not what I asked." I look up and she is now standing, laptop shut and forgotten. Her arms are crossed over her chest and her eyes are locked on mine like she is trying not to lose her shit. "You said this would stop," her voice trembles with controlled anger. "After the last time... after the last time I would expect you to learn your lesson about coming home like that."

"It's from yesterday. I didn't do anything today-"

"But what's going to be your excuse when it does happen again? When one of the kids sees the blood on your hands?"

"They won't. I told Killian I'm done but I have to do one last job in California-"

"You're leaving?" she asks, her voice cracking, making me look at her.

Her eyes are wide. "I didn't say-"

"You didn't have to." She laughs coldly and shakes her head. "God, Hayden. We just started to fix things last week. Things started to feel normal but then you leave practically all day. You end up seeing Killian more than the kids and I. And now you want to run away to another state to play mafia cleanup?"

"You think I want this?" I snap, turning off the tap. "You think I like sneaking around and coming home in someone else's blood? You think I don't hate lying to you?"

"Then stop!" she yells. "Stop choosing him over us!"

"I'm not choosing him," I groan and walk closer to her. "I'm just trying to protect you."

"By pushing me away?" she shoots back. "By making me lie to our kids about where their father is every single night? That's not protection Hayden, that's abandonment with a prettier coat." Her words cut deep, deeper than I wanted to admit. I stare at her, at the flush in her cheeks and the fire in her eyes, the pain beneath it all. "I told you before and I hope this is the last time I tell you but you're making me feel like I'm not enough for you Hayden. It's like you don't love me anymore."

I furrow my eyebrows and walk up to her, putting my hands on her face. "I do love you, what are you talking about?"

Tears form in her eyes and she backs away from me. "The Hayden I loved, wouldn't make me feel this way," she whispers. "I hate this. I hate who you've become when you're with him."

And that's when I snap.

I grab her by the waist and yank her against me, kissing her hard, not soft or gentle. It was messy and angry and laced with everything we didn't know how to say without starting a war. She fights at first, shoving at my chest and trying to push me away but her fingers curl into my shirt and pull me closer.

We're both breathing hard from the sudden shift and the echo of our argument in the air still. I should've just walked away and let us both cool down. But the second I saw fire in her eyes, red, rimmed, furious, and fucking beautiful, I snapped and couldn't control myself.

I need to feel her and have her in my arms and remind myself that she's still mine, I still have her.

She shoves me hard. "You think you can come home like that and just pretend it's fine?"

"No," I mutter, my voice low and rough. I back her into the wall and cage her there with my hands on either side of her head. "I think I need to shut you up before we both start saying things we'll regret."

"Fuck you," she spits.

I grab her face and kiss her like I'm starving. Like her mouth is the only thing that can burn away the rot and poison inside of me.

"You're so goddamn stubborn," I groan against her lips. "Maybe I need to fuck the attitude out of you."

She moans, even as her nails claw my arms. "Don't be gentle."

"I wasn't planning on it." I spin her around and shove her towards the bed. She stumbles, but doesn't get on the bed. She glancing over her shoulder at me. That look alone has my dick rock hard, throbbing behind my zipper. "

"And if I don't?"

"I'll fuck you right here." I walk closer to her, pressing my hips against hers. "But either way, I'm not leaving until you're begging me to stop."

She climbs on the bed slowly, like she wants to test me. Jaclyn pauses and looks back at me, her ass arched just enough to drive me insane. I lose the last bit of self control I have left and am on her in seconds.

I grab her hips and pull her back towards me. My mouth latches onto her neck and I yank her shirt up and over her head. "You missed this, didn't you?" I mutter as my hand slowly makes its way to the spot between her legs. "Missed me making you forget why you're mad?"

"I'm still mad at you," she hisses, her voice hitching as my fingers brush against her soaked underwear.

"Then take it out on me," I whisper in her ear. "Scratch me, bite me, tell me you hate me while I fuck you like you're mine."

"Hayden-"

"I said tell me," I say while rubbing my fingers against her pussy through her underwear.

"I hate how good you fuck me when I'm mad at you," she breathes.

"That's what I thought." I rip her underwear off, no time for slow. No time for sweet or gentle. I need to be inside her now. I shove my pants down just enough to free my dick, line up behind her and slam into her in one brutal thrust. She gasps, her fists clenching the sheets. "Take every inch like a good girl," I groan, rocking into her. "Even when you hate me."

"I don't-"

I shove her head into the mattress, cutting her off before I start going hard and deep. My hips slap against her ass with every thrust. My name falls from her lips between curses and muffled moans. Her body moves with mine, meeting me every time like she needed this as badly as I did.

Our anger was gasoline. Her body was the goddamn fire and I was burning.

"You're mine," I groan, gripping her hips tighter. "No matter how messed up we are, you'll always be mine."

She whimpers, collapsing slowly on her stomach. I lean over her back and press kisses to her shoulder blades, still thrusting slower now, deeper.

"Let me fix it," I whisper. "I'm going to fix this."

She doesn't answer, but she turns her head and catches my mouth in a kiss so raw it shatters me.

And when she cums, shaking and crying out my name, I follow. I cum inside her hard, clutching her like she was the only thing anchoring me to the fucking earth.

We collapse onto the bed, tangled and ruined.
Still angry.
Still broken.
But we're not walking away.
Not tonight at least.

Ten

Jaclyn

Hayden leaves today.

It's been a few days since we had sex and he revealed he was leaving.

I haven't said more than maybe ten sentences to him since then. All I can do is give him a disappointed look while he stares at me with longing and need.

I know I'm giving him a hard time and I should be spending these few days with him and enjoying him being here while I have him because who knows when or even if he'll be back but I don't want to think those thoughts.

Hayden's side of the bed is cold when I wake up, like it has been for a couple weeks with him getting up super early in the morning instead of me. Usually we get up together or I get up before him but lately he's been waking up early to take the kids to school and leaving to see Killian right after.

It almost feels like he checked out physically and emotionally.

I got through my morning routine with that pit in my stomach again, the one I thought was in the past. The one that used to live in me like a second heartbeat when things were at their worst.

Now it was back.

The constant overthinking and self doubt.

I walk downstairs and see the kids are already at the table. River has oatmeal smeared across her face, babbling nonsense as usual to her brothers while Easton tries to steal her spoon and Junior rolls his eyes at the both of them.

Hayden is in the kitchen with his back turned, packing his last protein bar into his duffle bag on the island. I saw three bags near the front door, black, heavy, and filled with God knows what.

Seeing the bags near the door feels like a goodbye I don't want to accept.

He glances over when I walk in. "Morning, princess."

I don't respond. I can't. If I open my mouth, the anger might spill out before the kids finish their breakfast and I don't want them seeing us argue, even though Junior and Easton notice it and have asked me about it.

River just notices that there is a shift between Hayden

and I but she can't really bring it up since her vocabulary is kind of short.

Junior catches on fast. "Are you leaving today?"

Hayden nods his head, coming over to ruffle his hair. "Yea, bud. Just for a little while."

"How long is a little while?" Easton asks, narrowing his eyes. He always needs specifics, structure. He doesn't do well with vague answers.

Hayden hesitates. "A few days. Maybe a week at the most."

Bullshit.

God knows how long he'll be gone or if he is even going to come back. And who knows if he's even telling the truth since all he's been doing is lying.

River drops her spoon and blinks up at him. "Daddy's leaving?" she asks, her little voice cracking.

My throat tightens and I force myself not to cry.

"Yea, baby," he says gently, picking her up and holding her against his chest. "But I'll be back before you know it. You won't even notice I'm gone."

Her little arms wrap around his neck. "I will."

God. My chest cracks in two.

He kisses the top of her head and hugs her tighter.

The rest of breakfast passes in tense silence. The boys eat slower than usual and River keeps glancing at the bags. I keep glancing at him, even though I don't want to. He isn't wearing his usual clothes like when he leaves for work. Just black joggers and a hoodie. Something easy to move around in.

After Hayden and I get breakfast cleaned, he says his goodbyes to them before sending them off to the living room to watch cartoons.

I stand by the front door while he stands by his bags. The silence stretches between us so thick I can barely breathe.

He looks up at me. "Princ-"

"Don't," I say, stepping back and blinking away the tears that are threatening to fall.

"I don't want it to be like this."

"Then maybe you shouldn't have made the same fucking choices that got us here."

His jaw tenses. "I'm doing this to protect-"

"Don't," I say again. "Don't pull the protection card. Not after everything we've talked about. You're not protecting us, you're protecting him. He's just using us to make it seem like you have no choice and you know that."

He steps closer, cautiously. "I'll call. I'll check in every day," he promises.

"Will you?" My voice cracks.

"Princess."

Tears slip down before I can stop them, hot, furious, and bitter.

"I can't keep doing this," I whisper. "I can't keep

watching you walk out like this. With blood on your hands and secrets in your pockets. I hate you for leaving."

His face breaks. "I know."

I step forward and grab his hoodie, yanking him down and kissing him like I'm trying to drown the ache. His hands grip my hips, holding me tighter than he should've, like it physically hurts to let go.

I pull away first. "Come back to me," I whisper. "Really come back. Not the half-alive version of you that's been showing up lately."

He nods his head, and presses his forehead against mine. "I will."

I want to believe him, I do.

But it's so hard when I'm so used to the Hayden who keeps leaving and not coming back with the Hayden I know and fell in love with.

He kisses my forehead before grabbing his bags from the floor. "I love you, princess."

"I love you, too," I say it back, because I know that there is a possibility he won't come back.

There always is.

Eleven

Jaclyn

It's only been a day.

Twenty four hours to be exact.

It's still loud in the house with the kids but it feels like something is missing.

For weeks, months, something has been missing and that's just Hayden.

I've been keeping myself busy today.

Cleaning, folding clothes, writing a little bit while the kids were at school, and taking River to the park.

The kids were my anchor, my distraction.

In the past I didn't want kids. I felt like having kids was going to be such a huge responsibility that I wasn't ready for.

I was barely able to take care of myself when I first had Junior.

I could barely take care of myself so how was I supposed to take care of kids?

I picked Junior and Easton up from school a few hours ago. I'm cooking dinner while they are in the living room.

Junior is laying on the couch watching some sort of fight on the TV, Easton is laying on the floor building legos, and River is at the table, drawing.

I'm grateful for them.

Grateful for the mess, the noise, the life they bring into me whenever I feel like darkness strikes. Because the minute they get quiet, my overthinking gets worse.

I try not to let them see it. The way I keep checking my phone, waiting for a text from him or the way I stared out the window every time a car drove by like maybe it was him and he came home early.

He hasn't.

I'm putting the kids' mashed potatoes on a plate next to the homemade Romanian recipe my mom gave me that has a red sauce and chicken with other seasonings.

"Mom!" Junior yells from the couch. I check to make sure the stove is off before I walk towards the living room, looking at Junior. "Look at the TV!"

I turn and look at the flat screen TV and see Hayden on the screen, in the middle of a boxing ring.

Hayden mentioned that he had a fight during his trip.

I wish I could have come to watch him, but I know this fight wasn't the only reason he went to California.

"Daddy!" River exclaims in the background.

I watch as Hayden wipes sweat from his forehead and breathes heavily into the mic someone gives him.

"Hayden! That was a great knockdown. You never fail to disappoint us. What would you like to say to your fans tonight?"

He licks the sweat falling on his lip and places one of his hands on his hip. "I'd like to thank my fans for the constant love and support they show me, in the ring and out of it. I'm glad that I'm able to do what I love for a living, it's a blessing."

"And I noticed your family isn't here with you tonight, they usually are. Anything to comment on that?" another interviewer asks.

He nods. "They're at home supporting me."

"Any honorable mentions tonight, Hayden?"

Hayden nods. "I'd like to mention my family tonight. I always do when I win fights but I want to honor my wife who is taking care of our kids at home, waiting for me to get home." He's looking straight into the camera, as if he's looking straight at me. "This win is for you, princess. All of my wins are. For every day you take care of the kids while I train or work. For every time you forgave me when I didn't deserve it. For loving the man underneath the bruises. You're the strongest person I know. Every time I step in the ring, I fight like hell to be worthy of you." Hayden exhales through his nose, his lips twitching into a soft smile. "I don't need a title or the rush. I've already got the only thing that matters waiting at home."

I stand frozen in front of the TV, my heart clenches so tight it's starting to hurt.

Junior grins. "He's talking about you, Mom."

I can't help but smile as I watch him on the TV. Reporters come closer to ask him more questions but he tries to get away.

The doorbell rings and River squeals, "Mama! The doorbell!"

I shake my head and walk out of the living room to go towards the front door.

And when I open the door, I freeze again.

They were everywhere.

Peonies.

Hundreds of them.

Soft pink petals overflowing from massive arrangements that lined my front porch like a fairytale exploded outside my house.

River comes out and gasps with a huge smile on her face. "Mommy! It's flowers!"

I blink. My throat goes tight and my heart clenches again.

There were more than just a few vases, there were boxes, wrapped bouquets, and baskets.

And in the very center of the biggest bouquet sat a white envelope.

My name is written in his handwriting.

I step outside barefoot, the cool breeze hitting my arms and the scent of peonies blooming around me like summer air.

I take the envelope and open it to grab the note inside.

I read the words to myself as the boys and River look at the flowers.

I know this doesn't fix it or my speech after my fight. I know you're still mad but remember you told me once, peonies are your favorite. They are rare to find and only come around once a year. Well, princess, you were a rare one to find and trust me I'm not letting you go. I'm not there but just know I haven't left you. I plan on coming back home, to our family, to you. I love you.

I grip the paper in my hand, heart in my throat.
Goddamn him.

"Who are they from?" Easton says, as he picks one flower up.

I swallow and tuck the note in my pocket before they can see the tears pricking my eyes. "Your dad."

River tiptoes over to one of the bunches and presses her nose to a petal. "They smell so pretty."

"Yea, they do," I whisper.

We spent the next twenty minutes hauling the flowers in the foyer. Junior helped with the heavier ones, Easton carried the vases with care, and River grabbed the ones from the floor while also naming every single bouquet.

I set the biggest one on the kitchen counter.

Right where I'd see it every time I passed by.

I pull out my phone and go to his contact. I send him one text.

> Thank you for the flowers, the note, and the speech. I love you. Please come back home in one piece so we can be a family again.

Twelve

Jaclyn

When I walk downstairs to the kitchen, I can't help but smile at the flowers filling every corner of the house.

The scent of peonies clings to everything, sweet, soft, and beautiful.

I brought one of the other vases and bouquets to my room on my side table so that I could wake up to them. I also put a vase in River's room since she said she wanted to have some of the flowers in her room.

When I gave River a bath this morning she begged me to put some of the flowers in her bath. She giggled and splashed water around which made me smile. I took some pictures of her, mainly for me and Hayden and for us to put around the house.

Junior is on the couch playing video games with Easton as I hold River in my arms.

"Morning, Mom," Easton yells when he sees me. "Are you making breakfast now?"

I roll my eyes.

This kid and his fucking breakfast.

Natalia texted me that she is stopping by today with Lilah since she took a trip here while Chris is practicing for the season. Natalia usually comes to Italy whenever Chris is busy with training.

"Yes, I'm making breakfast. Remember, Lilah and your Aunt Natalia are coming over."

"Down, mommy, down." River moves in my arms so I let her go and she runs to her brothers, probably going to beg them to play with her.

When Lilah comes over they'll probably play outside or video games inside.

Lilah is about the same age as Junior since Natalia and I were pregnant around the same time which was right after I left Arizona to move back in with my mom for a little bit.

It's the second day without Hayden and I hate how much I miss him.

I make breakfast sandwiches for the kids. For River I just make her eggs and bacon since she makes a huge mess whenever she eats a sandwich, but at the same time, she makes a mess with everything.

I clean up after breakfast and the kids go back to the living room to play games.

As I'm just finishing cleaning up, the doorbell rings.

I place the rag on the counter and go to the door, opening it.

I smile when I see Natalia's bright smile with Lilah standing next to her.

After all these years, Natalia still looks like she could pass as a college student. Her bright and wide smile, light eyes, and blonde hair, make her look so full of life and young.

"Natalia!" I wrap my arms around her and she wraps hers around me.

"Ohhh, Jaclyn! I've missed you so much, you have no clue, it's been so long," she squeals when she hugs me back.

She walks inside the house with Lilah. "How are you doing, pretty girl?" I ask Lilah.

She looks just like Natalia with her long, bright, blonde hair. But she is a combination of Chris and Natalia and as she gets older she is for sure going to be having all of the boys after her. Chris better watch out for her.

She shrugs. "Good, just have school going on," she says, not with excitement though.

"The boys and River are in the living room," I tell her and she walks away leaving Natalia and I in the foyer.

"You have so many things to tell me." Natalia wraps

her arm around my shoulder as we walk towards the dining table so we can sit and talk.

I pour a glass of wine for Natalia and I since we always drink wine together whenever we are catching up.

It's been a couple of months since I last saw Natalia. She usually visits once or twice a year. Or during the summer we travel to California, Utah, or New York to visit family, including Natalia.

I would say she is still one of my closest, if not, my only friend.

I do still talk to Max and Kayden from time to time.

Or if Hayden has fights throughout the year, depending on where the fight is, we'll go with him so we can see family and friends from college.

"How have you been?"

"Good, nothing much has been going on. Chris has been busy with practice and Lilah is at school all the time. So I haven't been doing much." She shrugs. "Now you have to tell me about you. You always have something going on, whether it has to do with Hayden, you're insane mom, or the three kids you have under your roof." I take a sip of my wine. "Tell me what's going on," she insists, looking more worried than happy now.

"It's just starting again," I whisper. "The late nights, the blood, the lies. I thought we were past this but he keeps going back to Killian. He keeps choosing that world over me and I feel like I'm not enough anymore."

Natalia's face softens. "You think he's choosing that over you?"

I shrug. "I don't know. It just feels like we fight and make up and then it happens again. Like I'm waiting for the next late night or lie. The next time he comes home looking like he just came from war."

"And the flowers?" she asks, looking around at the flowers that are in every corner of the house.

I smile, looking at all of them. "A peace offering. A beautiful, dramatic, expensive apology."

Natalia smirks. "Classic, Hayden. Always doing the most."

I laugh and shake my head. "Yea but it's not enough. I need more than a grand gesture. I need consistency. I need him, not the version of him that shows up after the damage is done."

She gives me a sad smile and traces her finger along the rim of her wine glass. "You've always been stronger than everyone I've ever known. You don't always have to carry all of that. Hayden should be there to help you carry it and lift some weight off your shoulders."

"It just feels like with Hayden, it's never easy."

"Life is never easy. Love is never easy. You and Hayden fought through hell for each other. He loves you and would probably die for you as you would do for him. You both created a beautiful, happy, and healthy family. Hayden right now is lost, but he's slowly finding his way back to you it looks like," she says, making me look at all of the flowers surrounding us.

"I hope you're right."

"I know I'm right." She smiles. "And until he comes back, you've got me and wine and Lilah terrorizing your son."

I crack a smile through the lump in my throat.

"Thank you, Nat."

She rests her hand on mine and squeezes softly. "You're my best friend. I'm always going to be here for you."

Thirteen

Hayden

Just one more job and I'm done.

One more job and I can enjoy the rest of my life with Jaclyn.

My ribs are throbbing, deep and aching pulses with every breath or movement. My knuckles are still crusted over from the fight last night.

I'm driving to one of the locations that Killian sent me. I guess this is where the thief is who has been stealing from him. He wants me to handle it, kill him.

My hands keep clenching around the steering wheel as I drive over to the location.

Jaclyn texted me last night telling me to make it home to her and our kids. I texted her back saying that I promise I will and nothing will stop me from coming home.

This mission isn't complicated.

I've gone on more complicated missions before so this is nothing.

I'm driving through East Oakland in a blacked out M4. Something quick to get away in and run from the cops since guns will go off.

I have a Glock on the passenger seat of the car.

My nerves are suddenly sky rocketing as if this is my first time doing a kill.

My ribs are in fucking pain, I want to go home to my kids and wife, and I am fucking anxious as hell to go in there. I just have this gut feeling that this won't be a quick and clean kill like I agreed with Killian.

When I get to the location I park the car in a safe spot. I step out into the California heat, air thick with grime and city sweat. The building I parked in front of looks abandoned, tagged up and hollow but I knew better. People like Craig, the person who is stealing from Killian, like hiding in the shadows.

I climb up the stairs, fast and silent. The door is already cracked open and that should have been my first red flag but I ignore it.

I pull out my gun from my waistband and hold it up as I slowly walk inside.

The place is trashed, overturned furniture, broken bottles, white powder and needles on the floor.

"Been waiting for you to finally find me." Craig walks out of the rooms in the hallway. Craig is an older guy, balding already and he has a nice, clean suit on. Killian always liked hiring clean and decent looking people to work for him since he says that appearance goes a long way and it pays off. "I thought Killian would have come to send his goodbyes."

"I'm not here to play games. We both know why I'm here. You've been bleeding Killian dry, slowly but enough for him to notice. I don't know if that makes you ballsy or stupid."

He shrugs. "Killian has enough money to wipe his ass with gold. What's a few hundred grand?"

"You think this is about the money?" I raise an eyebrow at him. "It's about loyalty."

Craig tilts his head. "Funny coming from you because word is that you want to walk away."

"I didn't come here to talk." I pull back the chamber.

"No, you came here to die, apparently."

His hand moves fast, drawing his gun from his waistband. But I'm faster. I duck sideways as the first shot rings.

I take cover and fire my gun at him. The bullet grazes him as he winces. He covers his arm with his hand and that's when I come out and shoot him once more in the chest.

He falls to his back, wincing and crying out in pain.

"You made the wrong choice and because of that, you'll die." Craig smirks while looking up at me as he puts pressure on his wounds, his gun laying to the side.

"What's so funny?" I ask, resting my foot on his chest and putting pressure where his heart is located.

"You didn't scan the house."

I furrow my eyebrows after another shot rings in the air.

Pain explodes through my stomach, like fire spreading across my skin. My breath punched out of my lungs as I stagger back, clutching my stomach. Blood soaks through my shirt, hot and sticky.

I turn and see a guy, someone who was helping Craig.

I drop to one knee, the gun still in my hand as my vision blurs.

"You chose the wrong team, Night," the guy says as he raises the gun to me.

I don't think twice before shooting him. His eyes widen as I pull the trigger, once, twice.

He crumbles like a puppet with cut strings and he falls to the ground.

I fall back, the world tilts sideways.

Jaclyn's face flickers in my mind, soft and angry, beautiful and tired. I think of the flowers and the note I sent her.

"I plan on coming back home to you."

I want to believe that.

I grab my phone and take deep breaths, struggling to keep my eyes open as I go to the first contact I see.

Rowan.

I click his contact and the phone rings before I hear his voice on the other end of the phone.

"About time you take my calls, fucker."

"I've been shot, you idiot."

"Fuck, where are you?"

I hear his voice muffle before everything goes dark.

Fourteen

Jaclyn

River squeals with laughter with a plastic tiara crooked on her head as she jumps around the living room with her stuffed unicorn.

Junior and Easton are on the couch, playing Mario Kart, yelling at the TV, their voices overlapped with chaotic joy. I'm on the couch with my legs curled under me, smiling to myself while working on my laptop.

I have written two chapters today despite all of the noise and chaos happening.

It's been a day since Natalia came over with Lilah. They are staying in a hotel nearby although I told them they are more than welcome to sleep over in the guest room. But they already got the hotel booked and they didn't feel like canceling it.

I haven't heard from Hayden since he texted me late

last night. He said that if everything goes well today, he should be home tomorrow and all I'm thinking about is having him in my arms again and being the family we were before he got involved with Killian again.

Things were pretty calm today, the usual calm at least in my opinion.

Natalia and Lilah are coming over tonight for dinner but until then, the kids kind of just did whatever they wanted today which was play video games and for River it was just running around the house and begging her brothers to play with her.

My phone rings and I look down to see if it's Hayden.

It's not, it's Rowan.

I stare at it for a second too long, heart doing that tight, painful squeeze as if something is wrong.

Rowan never calls unless it's to see how me and the kids are doing or if it's regarding Hayden.

"Hey," I answer, trying to sound normal like my stomach isn't already shrinking.

"Jaclyn." His voice is calm, too calm. "Hayden's been hurt."

Everything around me drops out of focus.

"What?" my voice cracks.

"He was shot. In the stomach. He's stable but unconscious. He's at a hospital here in Oakland. I thought you'd want to know right away."

I move my laptop and get up from the couch. "Is he-" I can't get the words out as my lungs tighten.

"He's alive, just in a light coma. Doctor says it's a waiting game now."

"What happened?"

Rowan sighs. "He called me last night, sounding like he was in pain. I called Killian and got a flight here with him. He's been sleeping since I got here."

"Killian's there?" I ask, my hand clenching the phone in my hand.

"Yea."

"I'll be on the first flight there."

Rowan is about to argue but I hang up on him.

My body moves on autopilot and I dial Natalia's phone number.

She answers on the first ring. "Hey," she answers, in her usual cheery tone.

"Hey, Hayden's been shot in California. I'm taking a flight there right now. Can you-"

"I'll be over in twenty minutes."

I force myself not to cry. "You'll stay with the kids for me?"

"Of course. Go be with my brother and make sure he stays alive and comes home. I'll grab my bags and check out of the hotel early for you."

"Thank you, Nat. I appreciate it a lot, seriously. You have no clue." I hang up and go to the living room.

"Kids." All three heads turn to me, confused at the tone in my voice. "Natalia is going to be staying here to watch you guys while I'm gone."

Junior furrows his eyebrows. "Why? Where are you going?"

"California. Something happened."

"Is it Daddy?" Easton asks, his voice too sharp for his age.

I freeze for a moment. "Yes, he's hurt. But he'll be okay."

"You're leaving us?" Easton's face crumples.

"No, no. I'm not leaving you guys forever," I say, walking towards them on the couch. "I just have to go see your dad and Natalia and Lilah are going to be staying here for a little while until I get back."

"But I don't want you to leave," River shrieks, starting to cry.

"Me too," Easton chimes in, getting up to hug my waist with River. "We want to see Daddy."

"I know, baby," I say, my throat burning. "But he's in the hospital right now. You can't be there. I need you guys to be brave for me, okay?" I look at River and Easton as they hug my waist.

"You always say we're a family but why can't we all go?" Junior stands, his jaw clenched looking just like his father.

"I am doing this for our family. I need to go and make

sure your father is okay and make sure he gets home. We'll come right back, I promise. I never broke a promise to you guys." Easton and River let go of me and look at me with tears in their eyes, breaking my heart to pieces. "Here." I hold out my pinkies to them. "I promise you guys that I'll be back and with your father." Easton and River hook their pinkies around mine and I lock the promise with my thumbs pressing theirs. "I need you guys to be good for Natalia, okay?"

"Yes, mommy," Easton says, trying to hold in his cries.

"You guys promise me to be good for Natalia while she watches you guys? I don't want to get any phone calls from her telling me that you guys are acting out of control while I'm gone."

"Okay," Junior says.

I look at him and rest my hands on his shoulders. "You are the oldest. You know better and I need you to watch your sister and brother and make sure they act right with Natalia while I'm gone. I swear I'll be back within the week and I'll call every single day or minute if you need me to. I just need you guys to be good while I'm gone, okay?"

They all say yes before River hugs me again, crying.

This will be the first time I leave River.

Since she was born she's always been by my side or Hayden's side so I know she's taking this hard. "Natalia will be here soon so I'm going to go pack okay?" I stand up with River still in my arms.

"Okay, mom," Junior says, not sounding happy but he gets it.

He knows it's probably serious.

He's a smart boy.

I go upstairs with River still crying in my arms. I set her down on the bed and try to calm her down while I pack a quick bag.

I try not to cry to myself as I pack, the worry and over-thinking getting to me. My heart splits because I have to leave them but also go to Hayden because he needs me.

I don't even know what I'll find when I get to Hayden.

But I know one thing.

I can't lose him. Not after everything we've been through together.

Fifteen

Jaclyn

Hospitals always smelled like antiseptic, panic, and sadness masked under a layer of lemon scented cleaner.

I hate them.

I always have since I was a kid.

The long waits, the needles, the bad news some people get here.

I got news that I wasn't going to live a completely normal life. I was going to be watching over my blood sugars every day for the rest of my life and pricking my finger or giving myself insulin.

I hate hospitals.

I didn't stop walking, didn't even pause at the front desk except to flash the room number that Rowan texted me. I moved on instinct, like my body knew where to go even though my heart had been screaming since my phone rang about thirteen hours ago.

It's the middle of the day here in California. I was on a plane for about eleven hours and it felt like the longest flight of my life.

Rowan tried calling me and texting me, saying that I didn't need to come to California and that he had it all under control, but nothing could have stopped me from coming to see Hayden.

Hell, I still have my duffle bag with all of my clothes because I couldn't afford to not stop by the hospital first to see Hayden.

I stand in front of Hayden's room door and take a deep breath.

Room 307.

I grip the handle and push it open.

Hayden's here.

Lying still.

Too still.

Machines hum softly, wires connected to his chest, a small beeping sound confirming that his heart is still beating even if everything else about him looks lifeless.

My throat closes.

He looks so pale and cold. He has bruises on his face and the white sheets around his waist make the angry red bandage across his abdomen seem even more violent. His knuckles are scraped and he has a cut on his eye.

But his face still looks the same.

Like Hayden.

Just asleep.

I walk up to him slowly. My eyes burn but I won't cry. Not yet.

"Hayden," I whisper, brushing his hair back from his forehead. "You're an idiot. An absolute idiot."

My hand lingers there, my fingers trembling. I want him to open his eyes. To smirk, to say something cocky or sarcastic. I would have taken anything from him at this moment.

Him threading his fingers in my hair and whispering, "It's going to be okay. I'm okay, princess." If it meant I don't have to stand here and feel this ache in my ribs like I'm the one who got shot.

The door opens behind me.

I don't have to turn around to know who it is.

Killian De Luca.

I can feel the air change, cold and smug and unwanted.

"Well," he says quietly, "I wasn't expecting you so soon."

I stand slowly and turn to face him.

Killian looks calm, collected and controlled like always.

Killian wasn't just dangerous, he was the kind of calm that came before a storm, beautiful, quiet, deadly.

"What the hell did you do?"

Killian doesn't flinch. "I didn't pull the trigger."

"No, you just pulled the strings, like always." My voice shakes with rage. "You sent him here, you knew this would happen."

"I didn't know he'd get ambushed-"

"You put him in the position to be ambushed." I snap, stepping closer to him. "You knew he had a family and someone waiting for him at home. Why did you let him join you again? Why couldn't you just turn him away and let him go?"

"I tried. But he came to me looking for a rush, a way to breathe. Hayden is the type of man that always needs action and a rush. I had what he needed."

"No, you just needed him to do your dirty work like always. You know right from wrong Killian, we aren't in our twenties anymore," I say. "You have a daughter at home." Killian glares at me. "I don't want to bring Luna into this but I will. What happens if you weren't able to go home to her? What would happen if you were shot and Luna had to wonder where her dad is and why her dad died? Why she doesn't have a dad to take care of her and love her anymore?"

"I didn't mean for this to happen-"

"But it did and I could have lost him," I say, my eyes filling with tears. Killian's eyes flicker to the bed before meeting my eyes again. "After everything I've been through Killian, I need him to keep me alive." I point to Hayden. "Him and my kids are the only reason why I'm here. I would have never been able to reach this point in my life if it wasn't for Hayden. He is everything to me."

We stand there, locked in a silent standoff while machines beep quietly behind me.

I know Killian understands what he did wrong and I know he feels empathy for Hayden because Hayden is his best friend or may be the only friend that he really has.

"You don't get to be here right now." Killian blinks. "I mean it, you don't get to play the grieving friend while he's hooked up to machines. Not when you practically handed him the fucking bullet."

Killian's mouth turns into a tight line. "You're angry, I get it."

"I almost lost the love of my life, Killian. I know you acted the same way with Reign. You should understand exactly where I'm coming from and how scared and pissed off I am."

Killian's jaw clenches and I notice his hands clench in a tight fists.

He nods before leaving without another word.

Sixteen

Hayden

Darkness had weight.

Not just the kind that pressed against your skin, but the kind that sat behind your ribs and stretched out until it wrapped around your spine and made it hard to breathe.

I feel like I've been floating in that darkness for what felt like years but then I heard her voice.

Muffled, sharp, fierce.

Jaclyn.

"I almost lost the love of my life Killian. I know you acted the same way with Reign. You should understand exactly where I'm coming from and how scared and pissed off I am."

I knew that tone. The one she used when her heart was breaking and she couldn't stop it from turning into anger. I heard it once, when we were in college and she was breaking up with me. She was angry but also heartbroken at the same time.

And now I'm hearing it again.

I try to move when I feel her hand touch my forehead.

A groan slips out before I can catch it and something inside my abdomen flares like fire. My whole body protests like it isn't ready to work again but I don't care.

"Hayden?" she whispers my name, soft and filled with desperation. Her hand cups my face, trembling slightly. "Hayden, look at me. You're awake."

I blink, the light above me makes my head throb but I force my eyes open.

"The lights," I mumble.

Her touch disappears, the light turns off before she returns and her hands are on my face again.

Jaclyn's hovering over me, her hair pulled into a low messy ponytail. Her eyes are glassy with unshed tears and her lips parted like she doesn't know whether to speak, cry, or kiss me.

I did it for her.

My hand found hers and I squeezed tightly. "You yelling at Killian again, princess?"

Her breath hitches and then she laughs. It's watery and full of disbelief.

"Oh my God." She leans forward and kisses my forehead and then my cheeks.

Her lips hover over my mouth like she doesn't want to hurt me. "Kiss me," I practically beg.

She smiles before leaning down and kissing me. I swear that kiss makes me instantly feel at peace and better.

It was a soft and desperate kiss, like she couldn't believe I was alive and here.

My forehead rests against hers when we finally pull apart, barely breathing, still burning. "I thought I was going to lose you," her voice cracks. "I didn't know if I'd get a phone call, funeral notice, or a closed casket. You can't do this to me, not again."

I swallow hard and my throat feels like it is coated in sandpaper but I force out, "I didn't want to leave."

"But you did leave. And look where it got you." Her hands move over mine, like she is grounding herself, like she needs to feel me to believe I'm real. "You don't get to just disappear into this mafia bullshit and hope I'll be waiting when you come home bleeding."

"I was trying to protect you."

"Bullshit," she snaps. "Don't give me that line. Protection doesn't mean shutting me out or risking your life and bleeding all over an abandoned apartment floor."

I close my eyes briefly. I hate that she is right, that this entire spiral started because I thought I could handle both worlds again.

I thought that the rush and my loyalty would be

enough but I learned the hard way that the only thing that matters to me is Jaclyn and my life with her.

I can't throw it all away just because of one rush.

"I thought if I just finished this one job..."

She stands and backs a few steps away from the bed. "There is always one last job, Hayden. There is always some threat or mission or 'I owe him' and I'm done competing with that. You're not just mine anymore, you're our kids'. You're River's hero. Her dad, that is supposed to always be there to protect her and her mom from the nightmares and the monsters." Her voice cracks as she tears up. "You're Easton's whole world. The person he looks up to. And Junior, he is basically a mini you. Why do you think I named Junior after you? You're literally his idol, Hayden. What am I supposed to tell them when you don't come home?"

The room goes quiet.

She sniffles and wipes her cheeks. "I can't do this again. I won't. So either you leave that life behind or I walk away like I did all those years ago. I don't want to, God, I don't want to but I will if I have to."

My chest aches worse than the bullet wound.

"Then I'm done," I say quietly. "I mean it, no more. No more side jobs, no more Killian, no more bullshit. Just you and the kids. That's it."

Jaclyn blinks. "You mean it?'

"I'm looking at the only thing that matters right now.

And it's not some loyalty to an empire I didn't ask to build, it's you."

She steps forward, her fingers brushing my jaw. I lean into the touch, even though the movement sends a jolt of pain through my abdomen.

"You scared the hell out of me, Hayden."

"I know," I rasp. "I scared the hell out of myself too."

I pull her down gently, our foreheads touching. She kisses me, slow and tentative at first then deeper, more desperate and passionate. She climbs into the hospital bed, curling against my side, being careful of my wound.

We don't say anything for a long time.

She just lays with me, her hand on my heart and my fingers tangled in her hair.

And for the first time in a long time, I let go of everything else.

Seventeen

Hayden

I took the first flight home after they cleared me from the hospital.

Jaclyn stayed with me the entire time, and didn't leave my side. Killian and Rowan came by but Jaclyn is the one who stayed every single second of every day I was under observation. Jaclyn and Killian barely talked. Killian made sure I was okay before he would leave the room.

I got the chance to finally catch up with Rowan since I've been ignoring his calls. He made a joke and said, "The only way to get you to call is if you are dying, shithead?" which I laughed at.

Jaclyn FaceTimed the kids and they were all happy to see me. Natalia and I chatted for a little bit as well.

But now I'm back in Lombardy, finally. It's been two days since I've been back home and when I walked through the front door I got attacked in hugs from my kids and even though the wound ached, I had the biggest smile on my face when I saw my kids because I thought for a second I was never going to see them again.

Jaclyn did all the right things when trying to take care of me but I told her I wanted her to relax and not worry so much.

She said, "I'm just happy that I didn't lose you."

"You will never lose me," I said before pressing my lips against hers.

Life has been calm and I've missed the calmness while I was off doing Killian's dirty work.

But that all stops today.

I sit across from him. He didn't offer me a drink when I showed up. Didn't crack a joke or make a jab about my aim being off.

He just stared at me with that same unreadable expression he'd perfected over the years.

"You took a bullet," he finally says, his voice low.

"No shit," I mutter. "Right under your name."

His jaw ticks. "You found the mole."

I nod. "He's dead." Silence stretches between us, heavy and final. "It wasn't clean or quiet. He put one in me before I could even finish the job."

Killian leans back in his chair and looks at me like he is doing the math in his head, weighing numbers, costs, losses.

"You're lucky you didn't bleed out."

"I did bleed out," I argue. "Just not enough to stop me from flying home in one piece."

His eyes narrow. "You're not here to debrief."

I shake my head. "No, I'm done."

His expression doesn't show anything. Almost like he saw this coming.

"You've said that before, Hayden." He looks at me knowingly.

"Not like this," I say. "Not when my wife has to tell my kids why I was in a hospital bed with a goddamn tube in my side. Not after seeing Jaclyn's face like she was so close to walking away from me."

Killian goes quiet again. The kind of quiet that makes men squirm. But not me.

I'm not afraid of him.

I know how he works and have grown closer with him and his family over the years.

Only thing I could ever be afraid of is losing the thing that is most important to me, and that's my family.

Jaclyn and the kids.

"I've done everything you've ever asked," I continue. "I've kept your secrets, fought your wars, and dragged myself home from every mission you threw me into. I did it out of loyalty and out of debt-"

"Don't lie to yourself, Hayden." He raises an eyebrow. "Everyone, even Jaclyn knows why you came back to me and that's because I gave you a reason to keep fighting. Fighting was never enough for you, you always needed and wanted more. You are your father's son."

"Rowan put a bullet in my father's head. I'm nothing like my father."

Killian stares at me for a moment too long.

Before he nods silently.

"I need you to make a promise to me."

"What?"

"If I beg you to come back you have to promise me you'll send me away. I can't lose Jaclyn or the kids and I can't keep going back to this life for a small amount of adrenaline. I need to have a calm life with Jaclyn. I've already put her through hell and I can't keep doing this to her."

"You really care about her, don't you?"

"She's the chaos and comfort. A storm and shelter. And every version of me that's worth saving lives in her eyes. I feel more than just love for her. I'm devoted to her for life."

Killian looks at me with pain in his eyes, like he understands.

He told me a little bit about his past relationship with Luna's mom. I know he gets it and he wishes he could have her to cherish and hold.

He's devoted to her even though she isn't here.

Before he can respond, his office door opens.

A small blur of black hair and pink barrels into the room.

"Daddy!"

Luna.

Killian's daughter.

Almost eleven years old and the only person in the world who can make him look soft.

"Luna, che fai qui, amore mio?" he asks, turning towards her. His voice lowered into something warm. Almost gentle.

"I drew you something." She beams, holding up a crayon-covered paper. "It's you, me, a doggy, and mommy."

Killian chuckles and pulls her onto his lap, brushing a strand of her hair from her eyes.

"I see. A ferocious guard dog?"

"No, silly. A snuggle dog."

I watch him as his expression melts with every word she says and for the first time in a long time I don't see a Capo. I see a father.

I've seen Killian and how he acts with Luna a bunch of times. He softens and acts like a person instead of a closed off asshole.

"You're a good one," I notice.

"I'm trying to be. For her," he says while staring down at her.

"I meant what I said Killian. I'm done." I stand.

He gives me another nod. "Then go home, Hayden. Go to your wife and kids."

And just like that it was over.

The empire, the job, the rush.

I leave it all in that office, with a little girl drawing snuggle dogs and a man who finally understands that we won't live in this world forever.

Eighteen

Hayden

The smell of sweat and old leather hits me the second we step into the gym.

It's not a fancy place, more grit than polish, more history than chrome. But that's why I brought the boys here. This is where I learned discipline, control, pain, how to throw a punch without losing myself in the heat of it.

It's been two months since California, since I got shot. Since I almost lost my life and didn't come home.

My abdomen still hurts a little bit but I want to get back into the gym and also show the boys what I do.

I have taken Junior to the gym with me in the past but since I'm not involved with Killian's business anymore, I want to spend more time with my boys, showing them how to properly channel their anger like I did.

I haven't been to this gym in a few years since I use my

gym back in Italy and I fly Freddie out to train me. Whenever I come to Utah, I come to visit family for a few days before leaving so I don't even have time to go to the gym and train.

Jaclyn is at my parents' house with River. I decided it was time to show my boys where I first got into fighting, the place that landed me where I am today.

If I never ran into this gym, into Freddie, then I wouldn't have ended up living with the Nights and I wouldn't be where I am.

Junior's eyes light up as he takes it all in. The boxing ring. The weight benches, the heavy bags hanging like ghosts waiting to fight. Easton clings onto my hand at first but eventually lets go, curiosity getting the best of him.

Junior has always liked it when I trained with him.

He thought it was fun and exhilarating.

Easton has always wondered what it's like training and now it's finally time I show him.

"You trained here?" Junior asks, craning his neck to look up at the rafters.

"Yea," I say, tossing my gym bag down. "Back when I was a little older than you, Carter used to drive me here everyday after school to meet with my trainer, Freddie."

"Uncle Freddie?" Easton asks, looking up at me with curiosity.

I nod my head. "He's the one who found me and took me to Carter."

"Was he mean?" Easton asks.

I smile a little. "Strict but he wasn't mean. Just didn't know how to show that he cared. He was figuring it out, like I am."

Junior nods his head, like he understood me while Easton just looked confused.

Easton is still young and trying to learn and keep up with how things work and what they mean while Junior is understanding and teaching what he knows to Easton.

I lead them to the mats and hand them each a pair of gloves. I drop to my knees between them.

I put the gloves on each of their hands. "Okay, so rule number one, fighting is the last resort. Not the first. You don't start fights, you finish them."

Junior nods his head and Easton mimics him.

The gloves on them were like twice their hand size and I know Jaclyn would want me to take a picture of them.

I stand and grab my phone. "Pose for your mom." I hold the phone up and take a picture as they pose in front of the camera like little badasses. I chuckle to myself and send her the photo.

"What's the next rule?" Easton asks.

I toss my phone to the side and start wrapping my hands as I say, "Rule number two is you protect two things. Your face and your pride. One with your hands and the other with your decisions."

"What's pride?" Easton frowns, trying to understand.

Junior answers before I can. "It's what you feel when you do something right, even when it's hard."

That's my kid.

But he's smart just like his mother.

I stand there and demonstrate the basics to him.

Their stance, guard, and jabs.

Junior knows the basics from my training with him before.

He is quick, he has my speed and aggression. He is strong and smart.

Easton is a little clumsy but determined. He fell twice trying to throw a cross but laughed each time like it didn't matter. As long as they are having fun I don't care. Watching them hit the bags with their tiny hands in over-sized gloves makes something in my chest twist.

They aren't growing up like I did, thank god.

I'm doing something for the younger version of myself because he wasn't able to have what I give these kids.

After an hour, they were winded and red faced but grinning ear to ear.

I give them both protein bars from my bag and ruffle their sweat-dampened hair.

"Are you proud of us?" Junior asks between bites.

I furrow my eyebrows at him. "Of course I am."

Junior nods his head before eating his protein bar again.

A flicker of Jaclyn showing because I know she would

ask something like that even though it's obvious how proud I am.

They both beam like that means the world.

We get into my Porsche and drive back to Carter and Alex's house.

I've had this car since college. I only ever drive the Porsche when I'm visiting since I keep it in the garage here.

It's almost sunset when we pull up to the house. The porch lights are on and River is outside barefoot in her pink summer dress running around in the grass, chasing bubbles while Jaclyn sits on a blanket with Alex. Carter stands a few feet away, sipping on a glass of what I'm assuming is whiskey.

I park the car and help the boys out. We make our way across the yard. Jaclyn looks up as we approach, her face softening the second she sees me.

"Hey, fighters," she says, Easton drops into her lap without hesitation. Junior sits beside her, still talking about his footwork and how he almost knocked a bag over.

His words, not mine.

I press a kiss to Alex's head as she stands and walks over to Carter.

I sit beside Jaclyn. "You should've seen him. Kid's got a wicked jab."

Jaclyn smiles. "I'm glad but just so we're clear, if either of them comes home with a black eye, I'm blaming you."

"Fair enough," I chuckle before pressing a kiss to her cheek.

She turns her head and connects her mouth with mine.

The world goes quiet when we kiss.

Me and her both smile into the kiss, like we can't get enough of each other.

River toddles over and crashes into my arms making me disconnect my mouth from Jaclyn's.

I pull her close and kiss the top of her head. "Hey my little princess, how was your night?"

"I played with bubbles, Daddy!" she squeals and I can't help but smile down at her.

She looks just like her mom.

I need to be careful with her, that's for sure.

I turn my head and look over at Carter.

He nods once and I know it's his way of saying he sees me, respects me, and is proud of me and the life I built even though I put him and Alex through hell.

Jaclyn leans her head against my shoulder as the sky turns a cotton candy pink behind us, the sounds of the kids filling the air like music.

For the first time in weeks, I don't feel torn between two worlds.

I only want one.

This one.

Nineteen

Jaclyn

Ten Years Later

The house is warm, glowing and loud with familiar chaos.

Junior leans back in his chair, running a hand through his dark brown grown out hair, his college hoodie wrinkled like he hadn't unpacked it since his flight. He looks like my baby still, the one I would hold when I would feel alone and cry when I was living in New York. He is taller now, and has put on muscle from working out.

He has taken on fighting like his father and plans on being a champion just like him, too.

Junior told us he has a girlfriend back in college. He would have brought her over but she's with her family this year.

He's growing up so much from the boy I raised and I couldn't be prouder.

"You are not cooking next year. We're ordering in." He points a fork at me.

He said I put too much seasoning in the chicken.

All I did was follow my mom's recipe but I guess I put too much seasoning.

"I underestimated my measurements. It happens to everyone." I roll my eyes at him.

Easton snorts from across the table, already halfway through his second plate.

He always loved my food, and would demand more food from me when he was a kid.

He's seventeen and still growing. His dark hair is messy in an artist or rebel look. He is wearing worn out paint splattered sweats and a hoodie from some art gallery in New York. My son, he got my creative side that's for sure.

He moved out at a very young age since he got into a private school in New York for art. He took up art in secondary school here and showed me his drawings and I told him he should go to school for it, especially if it makes him happy.

Easton never really got along with kids from his school and that's because they just didn't understand his mind.

But he's talented and doing great at school in New York. He visits whenever he can.

Hayden still doesn't understand how his son made a small career out of drawing, but God help anyone who criticizes him in front of his father.

"Mom's cooking isn't even bad. You're being dramatic." River rolls her eyes.

She's twelve now and fiercely independent.

She is still young and figuring herself out but she is doing great at school and has made a lot of friends for her age. I'm not worried about her, not yet at least.

She is curled up next to Hayden who is sitting beside me. She has one hand tucked into the crook of his arm and the other holding a mug of hot chocolate with extra marshmallows. Her curls are tied up in a messy bun and her voice has already started to change from that girlish tone to something more defined and confident which makes me proud.

I promised myself I would always make sure she is strong and only sees herself in a beautiful light instead of darkness like I had.

Hayden looks at our kids with a proud look on his face, almost like a 'we made it' expression.

He hasn't gone back to Killian, not once and life has been peaceful and beautiful. I stopped worrying and overthinking and he stopped lying.

He chose me, our family.

Killian and him are still friends but he doesn't do any favors for him anymore.

We made it.

After everything, we truly made it.

The night passes by in a blur.

The kids argue and we play one round of UNO before they go upstairs to their rooms for bed.

Hayden and I stay downstairs to clean, the lights are dim and I stand by the sink.

"You didn't let me help." He wraps his arms around my waist and whispers into my neck.

"You helped enough," I whisper back, leaning into him. "You cut the chicken and even managed to go through the evening without swearing."

"Personal growth." He shrugs.

I turn around in his arms and there he is, just as he's always been. Dangerous, tender, broken, and whole. A man who has been to hell and back with fire in his eyes and heart still intact.

And here I am, surviving everything we've gone through together.

"Did you see them tonight?" I ask softly, cupping his face.

"Every second."

"Junior has a girlfriend and is taking on fighting like you. Easton has such a creative mind with his drawing and he's doing really good in New York. And River is growing up into someone I wish I could have been when I was her age."

"I know, and I'm just thinking about how lucky I am that you didn't give up on me."

"You gave me reasons not to."

He looks like he's about to say something else but instead he just leans down and kisses me, slow at first, familiar, but it doesn't stay soft for long.

His hands slide down my hips, pulling me tight against him. I gasp in his mouth and he takes that sound as permission to deepen the kiss. He pushes me gently back against the edge of the counter.

"Everyone's asleep," he mumbles against my mouth, voice low.

And still after more than twenty years of being together, he still can't get enough of me.

Now that the kids are older and the boys are out of the house, he takes whatever chance he gets with me.

"Are you sure?" I ask, already breathless.

"Don't care."

He kisses me again, eager like we are still in our twenties, sneaking around and touching each other wherever we can.

He slides the dress straps from my shoulders slowly, too slowly, and he lets the dress fall to the floor.

"I should make you wait," he murmurs. Dragging his fingers over every curve of my waist. "For every time we had to stop, every time I had to hear one of the kids yell at us like we were criminals for touching each other."

I laugh breathlessly. "Then stop talking and take what you want already."

His eyes darken.

I don't even see it coming, just the way his mouth crashes into mine, tongue hot and possessive like he is claiming something that has always been his.

He picks me up and places me on the counter. His hands grip my thighs, fingers digging into the flesh as he yanks me to the edge of the counter. This time he doesn't hesitate.

"Every inch of you belongs to me and tonight I'm going to remind you exactly how much," he growls.

I'm already soaked for him.

He knows it too. He slides a hand between my legs and presses his fingers against my clit, through the thin lace of my underwear. I gasp and buck into his hand.

"You're shaking," he says, his voice mixes with reverence and cocky satisfaction. "God, you're so ready for me."

"You're cocky as ever," I rasp. "That hasn't aged a day."

He smiles, teasingly. "Neither has this mouth."

And then he drops to his knees.

Right there on the kitchen tile in front of the stove. He hooks his thumbs into the waistband of my underwear and tugs them down slowly, his eyes never leaving mine.

"You remember what I said the first time I fucked you?" he asks, his breath warm against my skin.

I barely choke out, "You said I was made for you."

His mouth curves into a sinful smirk. "That's still true."

Then he buries his face between my legs.

My head slams against the cabinets as I cry out, my fingers digging into his hair like I could hold myself there. His tongue moves with expert precision, slow strokes followed by sharp flicks. His stubble scraping the inside of my thighs, grounding me in the best way.

He moans against me and I swear that makes my stomach flip.

"Hayden," I whimper quietly, trying my best not to make too much noise. "If you keep-"

"I'm not stopping," he says roughly, dragging his mouth up to nip my inner thigh. "Not until you're dripping for me. Until you're shaking with need."

He delivers that promise.

He makes me cum twice on his face.

By the time he stands, my skin is flushed while my chest is heaving. I am practically begging him to thrust inside me.

He unbuckles his jeans with one hand and the other is still gripping my thigh

"Turn around."

I blink. "What?"

"Bend over the counter, now."

Something about the authority in his voice makes my entire body clench.

I slide down, legs shaky and turn, my palms bracing on the countertop with my hair falling in my face.

His hand grips my ass and slaps it. "If the kids weren't here, the things I'd do to this body." He then pushes into me with a deep, unrelenting stroke. I nearly collapse. "Fuck, princess," he rasps. "Still so goddamn tight, you're mine, you hear me?"

"Yours, always," I pant.

His palm covers my mouth as he thrusts into me harder, deep and punishing, like he had years to make up for, like every stroke is a love letter written in sweat and skin. His hands grip my hips, needing to anchor himself as he moves in and out.

"You take me so good, princess. Just like that. Fuck, just like that."

The sound of skin slapping echoes in the kitchen and I am praying that the kids won't hear or come down here.

I am gasping against his hand and clawing at the counter. He tilts my head up so that he can bite at my neck.

"You love when I fuck you like this," he whispers.

"I love everything you do to me," I moan quietly.

His movements stutter, cock tensing.

He is close.

With one hand still on my mouth, the other slides down between my thighs, he sends me over the edge with a flick to my clit.

"Come for me."

I shatter, my body trembling and legs barely holding me up as he follows me within seconds, groaning my name like a prayer.

We stay there for a long time, him still inside me, our bodies slick with sweat and tangled in the aftermath of something that felt like more than just sex.

Over twenty years of love and ache and chaos and devotion.

He pulls out and kisses my shoulder. He helps me stand upright and turns me around.

He looks at me with dark eyes and a rough voice. "I love you, princess." He grips my waist in his hand and pulls me closer to him.

"I love you, Hayden."

This is our forever.

No matter how chaotic or hard or messy.

We always find our way back.

THANK YOU

If you enjoyed this book please feel free to leave a review as it would mean a lot to me.

I always enjoy reading good reviews and I always love reading reviews that have criticism in them. Criticism makes me a better author and I always love knowing what I can work on as a writer.

A simple, "Great Book" would be amazing.

Appreciate your love and support so so much!

Acknowledgments

After writing so many acknowledgments you would think I know what to say.

Now this duet/series was suppose to end after Blinded By Hate but after knowing how much you guys love Jaclyn and Hayden I had to give them another small book.

I made this book mainly for you guys and I hope you all loved it. I know I probably gave some of you guys a heart attack.

As always thank you to my editor, Antonia for always sticking around and helping me and Ama, my cover designer and friend who has been such a help with this book and other books in the past.

Lastly, thank you to my readers for always supporting me and my dreams. I love you all endlessly.

About the Author

Jaclin Marie is a Self Published Author who lives in Southern California. When she isn't writing a compelling story or reading, she either spends her time at the gym or watching Disney Animation movies.

Jaclin started writing at the age of sixteen but she has always been a book lover. She started writing on this writing platform called Wattpad before she decided to publish her debut, Ace De Luca. Although that was her first published book, it wasn't the only book she has written. Since she started writing, she couldn't seem to stop and just like she found her passion.

Darkness evades Jaclin's mind and it demands to be heard. Writing darkness down on paper is something she loves doing. She makes her readers not only think about her plots but completely sob over them.

www.ingramcontent.com/pod-product-compliance
Lightning Source LLC
Chambersburg PA
CBHW030006010826
48973CB00009B/2685